THE MYSTERY
IN MEXICO

THE MYSTERY IN MEXICO

BY ANN SHELDON

WANDERER BOOKS

Published by Simon & Schuster, New York

Copyright © 1964 by Stratemeyer Syndicate
All rights reserved
including the right of reproduction
in whole or in part in any form
First Wanderer edition, 1981
Published by WANDERER BOOKS
A Simon & Schuster Division of
Gulf & Western Corporation
Simon & Schuster Building
1230 Avenue of the Americas
New York, New York 10020

Designed by Becky Tachna
Manufactured in the United States of America
10   9   8   7   6   5   4   3   2   1

WANDERER and colophon are trademarks
of Simon and Schuster

LINDA CRAIG is a trademark of Stratemeyer Syndicate

Library of Congress Cataloging in Publication Data

Sheldon, Ann.
Linda Craig, the mystery in Mexico.

Previously published as: Linda Craig and the mystery in Mexico.
Summary: While staying at the Quinta Floresta Ranch in Mexico where she
is to ride in a fiesta, Linda becomes involved in the investigation of the
mysterious disappearance of the ranch's water supply.
[1. Mystery and detective stories. 2. Mexico—Fiction]
I. Title. II. Title: Mystery in Mexico.
PZ7.S5413Lin 1981   [Fic]   81-2996
ISBN 0-671-42706-7   AACR2
ISBN 0-671-42703-2 (pbk.)

Contents

A Mysterious Disappearance 1

A trip to Mexico, an invitation to ride in an important fiesta, and now news of a mystery to solve!

It's almost too exciting to believe, Linda Craig thought.

She sat astride her beautiful palomino, Chica d'Oro, near the fence of the corral where she had been giving the filly a workout. Linda's grandfather, Tom Mallory, nicknamed Bronco, leaned against the fence. He had just brought her news of the mystery on the Mexican ranch she was to visit.

"Bronco, you say the ranch's water supply suddenly disappeared?" Linda asked.

"Yes. It's a very strange mystery. There is enough

water from a well to take care of the house, but the stream for the cattle and the great groves of olive trees vanished overnight."

Mr. Mallory looked up at the dark-haired, olive-skinned girl, whose big, brown eyes showed sympathetic concern and an eagerness to hear more. Linda, her brother Bob, and their close friends Kathy Hamilton and Larry Spencer had been chosen as representatives in a United States–Mexican Youth Exchange program. This had been set up so that young people, by living for a time across the border, would grow to understand the other country's customs, contribute what they could to help people there, and promote good feeling between them and their own countrymen.

The four Californians were to stay at Quinta Floresta, owned by Señor de Santis. In addition, the Craigs had received an invitation for them and their friends to ride in one of the outstanding fiestas.

Chica d'Oro suddenly tossed her head and whinnied. Linda patted her affectionately. "I believe you know what we're talking about, and you can't wait to go. Well, I can't either."

Bronco's face, ruddy and youthful despite his shock of iron-gray hair, and never serious for too long, now broke into a grin. "Linda, I told Señor de Santis that you and Bob are pretty good at solving mysteries."

Linda smiled. "I'll start on this one right now by

asking you a question. What was the source of this water supply that suddenly dried up?"

"A rushing mountain stream that ran through the many acres of Quinta Floresta and passed directly through the area where the house and outbuildings and olive groves stand. To have it suddenly vanish is unbelievable."

Linda had swung her knee over the saddle horn. She let Chica's reins fall loose so the filly could relax, and sat lost in thought. Finally she said, "Pedro and Josefina de Santis were coming up here to Rancho del Sol as exchange visitors. Will this problem make any difference in their plans?"

Bronco shook his head. "I called their father, and he said it won't. They will arrive here in a day or two."

"That will be fun," said Linda. "We can do some riding together before Bob and I leave."

She turned as her brother, eighteen, and two years older than Linda, rode up on his bay quarter horse, Rocket.

"Hi, Linda!" he called, reining in. Then he exclaimed to Bronco, "Boy! Am I glad that job of postholes for the back corner fence is finished! The ground up there is as hard as bedrock."

Bronco beamed at his tall, sandy-haired grandson. "That's a good job for one day. You'd better take the rest of the afternoon off. Kathy and Larry are coming over in a little while, anyhow."

Bob flexed his sore muscles. "Thanks, Bronco. These arms tell me I'm ready to quit work."

Linda was very fond of her brother, who favored the Scottish strain of their deceased father, Major Craig, while Linda had inherited the beauty of her late mother's Spanish ancestry. Their parents had been in a fatal accident in Hawaii a few months before. Linda and Bob had come to live with the Mallorys in Southern California. They had always thought of Rancho del Sol as a second home. They loved the exciting life on the quarter-horse and cattle ranch, which was often referred to as "Old Sol."

Bob looked inquiringly at Linda and Bronco. "You two having a private talkfest?"

"No," Linda answered, and Bronco told him of the telephone message from Mexico.

Bob frowned. "Surely there's a reasonable explanation. Maybe the water found a sinkhole as the Mojave River did here in the desert."

Bronco said thoughtfully, "If the stream had turned down into the ground, I'm sure Señor de Santis would have determined that himself. I have a hunch its disappearance may entail skulduggery of some sort."

"You mean somebody stole the water?" Linda asked.

"Could be," he replied.

Bob frowned again. "It's hard to imagine how

even a clever crook could make off with a rushing stream!"

Linda's dark eyes flashed at the thought. "If that did happen, I'd like to find the guilty person as well as the water!"

"Solving this mystery," said Bob, "sounds like a big assignment."

"I'm afraid it is," Bronco agreed. "And remember this—you'll be in a foreign country. Although Mexico is as close to the United States as merely stepping over a line, once you've taken that step you are on foreign soil. You will meet people whose customs and way of thinking will seem quite different from ours."

Linda's eyes twinkled. "We'll watch our manners, Bronco."

She told Bob about Pedro's and Josefina's expected arrival, then led Chica over to her stall and unsaddled her. Affectionately the girl laid one cheek against the filly's.

"We just *must* perform well in that fiesta, baby, so take good care of yourself." She hugged the palomino. "I want all Baja California to see my golden beauty and how splendidly she performs!"

As Linda rubbed Chica down, she wondered about Quinta Floresta. How different would it be from Rancho del Sol? She knew that the de Santises were wealthy and their house would be beautiful, of course. They raised cattle and horses in addition to selling large quantities of olives. A little chill went through Linda. If the water supply were not regained, those valuable trees would die!

That water didn't just poof off into thin air, I'm positive, Linda thought. Aloud she said, "Water, Chica. Do you think you could find water at Quinta Floresta?"

Chica nickered and gave Linda a shove with her nose. Linda laughed. "Oh, you! All you know about water is a drink when you're thirsty." She turned on the faucet over Chica's drinking pail in the corner.

Suddenly, both Linda and the palomino jumped as they heard a frantic squeal and the shriek of car brakes being slammed on. Linda ran from the stall to the back of the big, white, adobe house. The place had erupted into a state of confusion. After a moment's survey of the scene, she doubled up with laughter.

A huge, black Berkshire hog had escaped from its pen and run directly in front of Larry and Kathy, who had just arrived in a jeep. They had nearly hit the porker.

Cactus Mac, Old Sol's lean, bandy-legged foreman, was attempting to get a rope over the hog, which was running about frantically, looking for a means of escape. Rango, the ranch's yellow coyote-shepherd dog, was leaping up, barking excitedly. Luisa, the Mexican housekeeper, hearing the commotion, had hurried from the kitchen.

"You ornery critter!" Cactus cried. "Where do you think you're goin'—to market?"

Bob raced up from the pasture into which he had turned Rocket. He sized up the situation at a glance, sprinted to his saddle, which was hanging on the corral fence, and snatched his lasso from it.

"You old football pigskin!" he cried. "I'll fix you!"

Bob did not find this easy. No greased pig had ever evaded capture better than this tricky, running, turning, dodging sow. Her squeals were earsplitting. Cactus Mac was still trying to catch her, but having no luck.

Bob decided to try a new maneuver. He slyly moved in from a side position and neatly dabbed a loop over the hog, digging his heels in as he hauled the charging animal to a stop. Then he wrapped his prize up in the rope.

The amused onlookers clapped. "Good work!" cried Larry. "We'll put you in the next greased-hog contest!"

"Don't give me all the credit. Cactus had her pretty tired out," Bob said with a grin, and tossed the rope end to the foreman.

Cactus Mac's weather-tanned face broke into a wide smile. "Yes," he drawled, "I guess this critter's plumb worn out now an' a couple o' pounds lighter."

Laughing, the young people went up to the patio.

"For such a fat gal, that pig sure got around fast,"

commented Kathy, who was pretty, had big, blue eyes, honey-blond hair, and a keen sense of humor.

Larry, thoughtful and brown eyed, with rather unruly brown hair, said, "I had to stop so quickly I thought both Kathy and I were going to take a header right onto that hog's back."

"High on the hog, eh?" Bob exclaimed.

Larry groaned. "I ought to duck you in the horse trough for that one! But it might muss up that fancy yellow shirt of yours." Bob was needled a good deal about his collection of bright-colored riding and work shirts.

Luisa brought out a tray with a pitcher of orange juice, glasses, and a plate of homemade coconut cookies. The housekeeper beamed as she set the tray on a small, round table in the center of the group. In Spanish she said, "A little citrus and a little sweet—they are good for one, *sí?*"

"Everything you cook is good for me," Kathy answered, smiling, "just so long as you don't serve those burning red peppers!"

Luisa's black eyes sparkled, and she laughed softly as she hurried back into the house.

Larry and Kathy were told the news about the Mexican mystery. Larry whistled. "Sounds bad for the de Santises. And we won't have much time to solve the mystery. We're slated by the Youth Council to remain down there for only three weeks."

Kathy added, "We're about ready to start any time. Larry and I have Patches washed for the trip, and all her equipment cleaned and polished. So we're here now to help with Gypsy, Rocket, and Chica."

Patches was Kathy's pinto mare, and Gypsy an Old Sol roan mare that Larry rode when the four young people went on their junkets together.

"Everything's set," Bob answered. "Thanks just the same."

Rango had joined the group as soon as they had gathered on the patio. The dog had taken turns sitting before each person and raising a paw to beg a cookie. Finally he stayed in front of Linda, watching her face intently. Receiving nothing, he planted a big paw on her knee and gave a couple of sharp barks.

"Hey, you've had your quota," Bob said. "Leave some for us!"

Paying no attention to the remark, Rango gave two more short barks and two thumps with his big plume of a tail.

"I don't think it's a cookie he wants now," Linda said. "He senses that we're talking about going someplace, and he's putting in his reservation."

Bob gave Rango a long look. "Our clearance paper from the council to the border guard mentions four persons and four horses, but no dog."

"No dog" had an unpleasantly familiar ring to

Rango. He turned his head to Bob with a guttural protest, then switched back to Linda, giving another sharp, pleading bark.

Linda put a tender hand on his big head. "We'll see, boy. I'd really like to have you along—maybe it could be arranged."

Contented, the dog flopped at her feet.

"Animals are good at smelling out water," Larry said, and Rango thumped his tail happily.

The conversation turned to Josefina and Pedro. Kathy said dreamily, "I'll show Pedro the desert and—"

"Say, don't you two girls go into combat over that Mexican boy!" Bob warned with pretended severity.

"And don't you boys fall so hard for Josefina you won't want to go to Mexico," Linda countered.

During the evening, word came that the young de Santises would arrive the following morning by plane. Linda, Bob, and Bronco drove to the airport to meet their visitors. When the plane landed and Linda saw the Mexican girl coming in her direction, she exclaimed, "Josefina is just darling! And—her brother's great!"

The de Santises resembled each other. Both had soft, brown eyes; beautiful, dark, curly hair; and ready smiles that revealed even, white teeth.

With the brother and sister was a young man. Pedro introduced them all, adding, "Felipe Maranez is a *vaquero* on our ranch. He hopes to be asked to sleep in your bunkhouse, and look over the fine quarter horses you have for sale. My father wishes to buy some."

"Welcome, Felipe," Bronco greeted him heartily. "We're glad to have you join us."

The group arrived back at Old Sol near lunchtime. Kathy and Larry had come over and were preparing a barbecue in the patio. Larry was busy starting the charcoal fire.

Nearby sat a stately woman with graying black hair worn in the old-time Spanish style. She was Grandmother Mallory, always called Doña by Linda and Bob. Though firm and highly ethical in her ideals, she had endeared herself to everyone by her kindness and wise counsel. She greeted the visitors with a gracious smile and cordial welcome.

"We are very happy that you have joined us, and I hope you will feel at home on our American ranch."

Bob took Felipe to the bunkhouse and left him with Cactus Mac. Sam, the cook, had a big lunch ready for the men.

Linda, meanwhile, had shown Pedro and Josefina their rooms in the two-story ranch house. They came down a few minutes later to watch the barbecuing.

When all the food was served, Josefina, who was seated next to Linda, said, "Señor Mallory told our father that you are good at solving mysteries. Did he mean it, or was he joking?"

Linda smiled. "The four of us, Bob, Larry, Kathy, and myself have had some luck on cases."

"How thrilling!" Josefina exclaimed. "Since that is so, I want to give you all a very special message from my father about our mystery."

The Charro *and the Bull*   2

As the Old Sol group listened eagerly, Josefina went on. "My father is giving you four the exclusive right for a short time to try figuring out why our stream disappeared—that is, if you want to."

"Do we!" cried Bob.

"It's marvelous!" Linda burst out joyfully, while Kathy and Larry beamed their agreement.

Pedro looked at the Californians intently. After a short pause he said, "I wish you every success. Josefina and I are sorry we cannot join you, but we've given our word to the Youth Council to remain here."

Josefina's eyes were troubled. "My father is

dreadfully upset over the possible loss of his fine olive trees. He says they cannot live longer than two weeks more without irrigation."

Kathy gave her a sympathetic smile, then held up her lemonade glass. "Here's a toast to the successful outcome of this mystery. And *viva Méjico!*" They all joined her.

Linda was smiling too, but there was caution in her voice as she said, "This is such an important challenge for the four of us, I'll feel very bad if we don't meet it."

Bob picked up Linda's cautious note. "We are not graduate engineers. If the water problem falls into that category, we may as well stop before we begin."

Pedro shook his head. "My father called in two expert engineers when the trouble started. They could not arrive at an answer for the disappearance of the water or a solution for its return. They could only say that some unforeseen geological event must have taken place."

Doña Mallory looked at the young people with concern. "This is your strangest undertaking yet. There may be danger involved."

"We'll be careful," Linda promised. Turning to the visitors, she said, "Our group doesn't leave until day after tomorrow. That'll give us time to show Pedro and Josefina our ranch tomorrow."

"Wonderful," Josefina said enthusiastically. "Will

you have your famous filly Chica d'Oro do some of her tricks for us?"

Linda laughed. "Of course. Chica will love that. She's a real ham. Wait until you see her when she has an audience."

"And she loves the treats Linda gives her for doing her tricks," Kathy teased.

Pedro chuckled. "Our Felipe is a very fine *charro* and belongs to one of the *charro* clubs. Their competitions in Mexico are like your rodeos here. The Rancho del Charro in Mexico City is the finest of all the arenas."

"I've heard about the tailing of the bulls they do in their performances," Larry said. "What do you call it in Spanish?"

"*La Suerte de Colear*—the Tailing of the Bulls."

"Does Felipe do that?" Larry asked.

"He is one of the best."

"We must see him in action," Bob declared. "We have a couple of bulls out back."

Josefina suggested with a roguish smile, "I'm sure if Linda asks Felipe, he will show you how it is done."

Linda, blushing a little, agreed to do so, then said, "Please tell us more about the Mexican *charros*."

"They are Mexico's daredevil riders," Pedro responded with a laugh. "They all instruct their children in the arts of the *charros*, so that the skill and traditions will never die out. Their costumes and big sombreros are ornate and expensive. The performances are thrilling spectacles, with colorful dress, fast riding, and always singing and dancing."

"I can hardly wait to see one," Kathy said enthusiastically. "I only hope I can survive all the excitement!"

Linda told the de Santises that her group was scheduled to ride in a fiesta horse show in Mexico. "Will any *charros* be in it?"

"There are always some men competing in every horse event," Josefina replied.

"What specialties do the *charros* perform besides tailing the bulls?" Larry asked.

"Trick and fancy roping," said Pedro. "But instead of using different lengths and weights of cotton ropes for various tricks as your ropers do, they use just one long maguey rope.

"The *charros* also have beautiful fast-riding mounted *quadrilles*. They do the tricky forefooting, and the *paso de muerte*, which means pass of death."

"Sounds horrible," said Kathy. "What in the world is it?"

The listeners were intent as Pedro explained. "A *charro* rides his horse bareback at full speed around the circular arena in pursuit of a bronc. While going full tilt, he grasps the mane of the bronc, and passes from his own horse onto the other's back."

"You have forgotten about a very important

event," Josefina reminded her brother, giving him a playful tap on the arm.

Pedro looked puzzled for a moment, then grinned at his sister. "I suppose you mean the fast-riding-and-stops event for the young women, the *charras*. You describe it, Josefina."

"The girls ride sidesaddle," she said, "and are dressed in long, frilly, colorful dresses and big sombreros. They come into the arena at a dead run, ending in a wild, sliding stop. Then, with the aid of a small bat, they whirl and spin their horses like pinwheels. All the time they smile and laugh. It is very spectacular. You would love to be in it, girls."

Kathy exclaimed, "I'd be satisfied just to watch it. How about you, Linda?"

Her friend chuckled. "I might be tempted to try it."

Mrs. Mallory gave her granddaughter a worried look. Linda hugged her affectionately. "Just fooling, Doña dear," she said.

Bronco cleared his throat. "Pedro, you have me wanting to pack my bag and take right off for south of the border!"

"You would enjoy it," the Mexican boy said. "Some Sunday, visit the beautiful Rancho del Charro. It is the greatest show in the world."

"I'd like to know," said Kathy, "what the difference is between a *vaquero* and a *charro*. You said that Felipe was a *vaquero* on your ranch, but you also called him a *charro*."

"That is easy," Pedro answered. "The *vaquero* is the working hand on a ranch—the same as your cowboy," he informed her. "The *charro* is the performing rider, like your rodeo rider. All *vaqueros* are not *charros*, but most *charros* are *vaqueros*. You look puzzled, Kathy. Haven't I made it clear?"

"Oh yes," she said quickly. "To me, that isn't Mexico. I always think of music and dancing in connection with your country."

"You know Mexican dances?" Pedro asked, jumping up from his chair and running over quickly to the girl's side.

Kathy shook her head, but he pulled her up and swung her into a fast rumba. The others caught the spirit and began to clap in rhythm.

Finally Kathy sank into a chair, exhausted and breathless. "If that's typical of Mexico," she gasped, "I'll have to go into training!"

"I'd better get you home to finish your packing while you can still walk," Larry announced teasingly, and the two left.

That evening, after a trip around the ranch, Pedro and Josefina urged the Craigs to recount some of their past adventures. Linda and Bob showed them the color photos they had taken on various trips they had made since coming to live in California.

Josefina's eyes lighted up as Linda laid out the pictures of Indian Charlie's place, where she had found Chica; the cliff dwellers' location, where an old hermit nearly trapped them in a rock slide; the

Black Canyon, with its walls of petroglyphs; the Cortés cove with the three crosses; the turquoise deposits; the spectacular great condor; desert flowers; and other scenic views.

"It's a magic land," Josefina murmured. "I love it already!" Then she looked with deep confidence at Linda and Bob. "After all this, I am sure that you two and Kathy and Larry will solve the mystery of what happened to our Agua Vieja—that's the name of the lost stream at our Quinta Floresta."

"Thank you," said Linda. "I have a feeling we'll need lots of luck."

The next morning after breakfast, the Craigs and their visitors went out to the riding ring. Larry and Kathy drove in almost immediately.

Felipe, with his knowledge and love of good horse-flesh, stood by with a rapt expression as Linda led Chica d'Oro into the ring. The shining, golden filly tossed her heavy, white mane; arched her long, white tail; and lifted her small, dainty hooves high in a prancing gait, fully aware of the onlookers' attention.

"A beautiful animal," Felipe said.

Linda mounted her and took the horse about the ring in a walk, trot, and canter, and the four-mile and five-mile parade gaits. Then she put Chica through a figure eight and a pivot.

"*Olé! Olé!*" shouted Felipe, Pedro, and Josefina, and all the onlookers clapped.

Linda dismounted in front of Felipe.

"You are a very good rider," he complimented her. "And you have a fine young horse. You trained her yourself?"

"Yes, and thank you." Linda smiled and had Chica bow her gratitude.

Felipe's eyes glowed with admiration. He said, "I know a very wealthy man in Mexico, the director of the *Asociación Nacional de Charros,* who will pay you the filly's weight in gold."

Linda turned to Chica. "Do you want to be sold to the director of the *charros?*"

The palomino shook her head violently from side to side to indicate no. Felipe and the others laughed. Then Chica rolled back her lips and added a horselaugh of her own.

"I have never seen such a filly!" the *charro* exclaimed. "If you should change your mind about selling Chica, let me know."

Linda laughed. "Not a chance. And now, Felipe, we would all like to see one of your famous competitive feats," she said coaxingly. "Would you show us the tailing of the bull?"

Felipe shrugged. "I must have the bull."

Bob gave a wave of his arm. "*El toro* awaits!"

Cactus Mac, who had been told of the plan beforehand, stood with a couple of Old Sol cowboys near the farthest gate with a sturdy, little, red Hereford bull.

Felipe's dark eyes snapped. "That is a fine animal. I will get the quarter horse—one of those I picked yesterday to take back to Señor de Santis. He is a fast one."

While Felipe was bringing his horse, Linda returned Chica to her stall and gave the filly some carrot chunks from her pocket. "You are the finest, baby. That's what they all say." Chica immodestly nickered agreement.

Linda hurried back to the ring, where everyone was waiting eagerly for Felipe's appearance. As soon as he rode up on his horse, Cactus Mac turned the bull into the ring.

Felipe ran him to the fence, then turned the animal back toward the center, racing in pursuit. When he overtook the bull, Felipe grasped him by the tail, kicked his right foot over the tail, reined sharply to the left, and upset the bull.

"Bravo! Bravo!" The watchers shouted and applauded the swift, skillful, and dramatic performance. Smiling and bowing, Felipe rode from the ring.

"What a marvelous rider!" Linda exclaimed. "I could learn a lot from him."

Later, after a tour of the ranch in a jeep, the family and their friends gathered on the patio for a snack and talked of plans for the holiday in Mexico. It was decided that Larry would make a quick trip in one of the trailers to bring back Patches and his and Kathy's bags. The two would spend the night at Old Sol to facilitate an early start with the Craigs in the morning.

Rango again began his pleading to Linda to go on the ride as he watched Cactus Mac stow gear in the trailer compartments. Even a juicy roast-beef bone failed to distract him.

Linda stroked his big head tenderly. "I'd like to take you along, Rango, but I don't believe we can get you across the border. The authorities would surely stop us."

Rango cocked his head and studied Linda with an odd look.

"Don't make me feel like a meanie," she told him. "Those eyes of yours will have me weeping in a moment!"

That evening Pedro brought out his guitar, which he strummed with his fingers as he and Josefina sang several appealing Mexican folk songs.

Bob played his guitar with a pick while Linda, Kathy, and Larry sang some cowboy tunes. The visitors were amused at some and kept asking for encores. Bob finally did an original number about a gopher outwitting a fox.

Doña sighed happily as good-nights were finally said. "This will always be a memorable evening," she murmured. As Linda and Bob kissed her good-night, she said, "I shall miss you very much."

"We'll be back before you know it." Linda gave Doña a hug.

By six o'clock the next morning, the four riders were ready to travel. As was customary when they went on trips, Chica and Rocket rode in the palomino's trailer, with Gypsy and Patches in the other. Larry drove Linda in one car, and Kathy accompanied Bob in his.

Doña, Bronco, Luisa, Pedro, and Josefina stood on the patio waiting to wave good-bye. Rango was nowhere about.

Bronco asked with some concern, "Where can that hound be? He's always right here rarin' to go with you young folks."

"Or sitting on his haunches looking reproachful if he can't," Kathy remarked.

Bob said, "Rango's often out back with the cattle early in the morning. Perhaps that's where he is now."

Bronco shrugged. "You'd better get started," he advised. "I must go down to the stockyards on an errand today. I'll take Rango along. That'll keep him happy."

Good-byes were said, and Josefina called pleadingly, "Solve the mystery soon!"

The Old Sol foursome, promising to do their best, rolled away. It was a crisp, sunshiny morning, perfect for travel, and they felt a tingle of excitement for this new adventure.

At midmorning the travelers stopped at a roadside stand to stretch and have a snack. By noon they had arrived at the Mexican border south of San Diego. Two polite guards greeted them.

Bob handed one the paper prepared by the Youth Council arranging for the clearance of the four young people and their horses. At the other guard's request, Linda and Larry went around back to open the endgates. As they did, a great flash of yellow fur sprang out from Chica's side.

Rango! The dog leaped around Linda with joyous barks.

The surprised guard with the paper asked, "Is this animal cleared also?"

"Oh, Rango!" Linda gasped. "Your name isn't on the clearance paper. What shall we do?"

Rango answered that question in short order. Like a shot he bounded across the border into Mexico and disappeared in the chaparral!

A Spy? 3

Linda was frightened. The inspectors might think that she and her companions had deliberately tried to sneak Rango into Mexico without declaring him. The officials could turn back the whole group because of it!

Bob, Larry, and Kathy were speechless with surprise and worry. Someone must say something to save us all, Linda thought. She took a deep breath and tried to appear calm as she explained.

"That was our ranch dog, Rango. We didn't know he was along. He always goes on trips with us, if he can, but we hadn't planned on bringing him this time."

The faces of the border guards did not change expression.

"He stowed away," Linda went on desperately. "He must have jumped into the trailer when we weren't looking, and apparently was lying curled up between my palomino's feet. The horse and the dog are great pals."

The inspector who held their clearance paper suddenly smiled at Linda, then shrugged. "That is a foxy dog. You go on, and do not worry about him. We will have him picked up and held safely at an animal shelter until your return."

"Oh, thank you!" said Linda and Bob together.

As the foursome continued their journey, Linda sighed. "What a horrible thing for Rango to be shut up in a cage for three weeks!"

Larry gave her a slow wink. "You don't really think Rango is going to let anyone nab him, do you? He's probably keeping pace with us out there in the brush. Watch carefully."

It was only a little farther on that they saw a heavily panting Rango seated in the middle of the road waiting for them. Linda gave an exclamation of joy. Both outfits pulled to a quick stop, and all four young people jumped out.

There were a riotous few moments of greeting. Then Linda scolded, "You're a bad dog to pull this trick and worry us half out of our wits." But she could not help hugging Rango in her relief at having him safely with them again.

Rango opened his mouth in a great yawn and joyously waved his tail.

Kathy giggled and struck a pose. "Mexico, land of mystery. Disappearing water. Reappearing dog."

"Maybe this is a good omen," Linda said.

"It would be a good omen if a sandwich could appear right now," Kathy put in. "I'm starved."

Bob said the little village of Pesca was only a couple of miles ahead. "We'll stop there for lunch and get some food and water for Rango, too. That was a long, hot run for you, old fellow."

"It's hot, period," Kathy muttered.

The travelers climbed back into the cars, with Rango seated between Linda and Larry. When they reached the edge of Pesca, the hungry group obtained sandwiches and bottled soda at a counter restaurant. An outside faucet at one side of the building dripped into a crock basin. Rango drank thirstily, then lay down on the cool, damp ground while the others ate. When Linda finished she brought him some pieces of baloney, which he gobbled greedily.

"Let's go!" Bob called.

When they started off again, Rango took his place with Linda and Larry in happy triumph. "You'd better behave yourself and earn your way down here," said Larry, nudging the coyote-shepherd. "Right now you're supposed to be in a dog pound at the border."

Rango's big tongue came out and licked Larry's cheek. Then he settled down.

The caravan now was well into Baja California,

with its rugged red and green hills chuting down onto the plains, which were under cultivation with many different vegetables.

"See those gray-blue maguey plants on those high fields?" Larry pointed out to Linda. "Their fibers are used in millions of bags and mats, baskets and ropes."

On either side of the travelers stretched fields of beans of many varieties. Linda knew that the natives consumed these by the ton. Here and there also lay patches of corn.

"Corn is mainly used for tortillas, the Mexican's favorite food," said Larry.

Away to the west stretched the turquoise ocean, slapping its foam-crested waves onto white sand beaches.

"This is lovely," said Linda. "We must plan on some swimming while we're here."

Darkness had just fallen and the moon was rising when the travelers arrived at their destination. Bob led the two outfits into Quinta Floresta. The beautiful, broad entrance road was edged with scarlet-flowered fire bushes. Far to one side could be seen the great groves of grayish-green olive trees.

The Quinta Floresta hacienda had a rambling adobe house whose color had mellowed to a soft gold. Over the broad, deep windows were brown spindles ornamented in blue, red, and green. Leading away from it were two flowering, vine-covered porticoes.

"How exquisite!" Linda exclaimed.

A floodlight illuminated the house entrance, with its big, open, wrought-iron gates, huge, brilliantly hued pottery jars, and border masses of pink Mexican primroses. On a bronze perch nearby sat a regal white cockatoo with a bright yellow crest.

Having heard the outfits come in, Enrique and Yolanda de Santis hurried outside to welcome their guests. Señor de Santis was a tall, dignified, white-haired man with warm, brown eyes. His wife, a slim, charming woman, had sparkling, dark eyes. Her black hair was swirled in a chignon on top of her head. She wore an elaborately embroidered, bright blue Mexican cotton dress and several bracelets of hand-carved silver.

"I am delighted that you made the journey safely," she said, smiling. "It must have been a long, hot ride."

Although Señor de Santis's welcome was less effusive, it was sincere. But his face showed his deep concern over the big problem of Quinta Floresta.

"It is very kind of you to entertain us," said Linda. She smiled. "We already love Josefina and Pedro."

The conversation was interrupted by Rango, who had just noticed the white cockatoo. Beside himself at the sight of the strange bird, he jumped up at it and barked. The cockatoo fluttered its wings excitedly and responded with a raucous scolding. Incensed, Rango leaped about the perch, trying to reach the bird.

"Rango! Stop that! Quiet down!" Linda cried, grabbing the dog's collar and attempting to pull him away. She said apologetically to the de Santises, "Rango stowed away in the horse trailer. We didn't plan to bring him."

Linda was surprised to see their hostess smiling broadly. "This is a magnificent dog. He is welcome. Let him loose and do not worry. Prevenido can take care of himself."

"Prevenido?" repeated Linda. "That means 'on guard.'"

"Yes, it does," Señora de Santis replied. "You speak Spanish?"

"Linda and Bob speak it fluently," Larry informed her. "Kathy and I aren't so proficient."

With some misgivings, Linda let Rango loose. Taking that as assent to his former actions, Rango jumped at the cockatoo again and barked. With a shriek, Prevenido swooped off his perch and gave the dog a hard peck with his sharp beak.

Rango fell back with a yelp. The beautiful, white bird returned to its perch and calmly preened its feathers. The shepherd dog eyed Prevenido, but did not bother the cockatoo again.

"I think there will be no more trouble." Señor de Santis chuckled.

He rang an outside bell, and two smiling *vaqueros* appeared from the shadows. The visitors' host said, "These boys will take your bags. Then they will show you the stables and help you with the horses. As soon as you have returned to the house and freshened up, we will have dinner."

It was nine o'clock when Linda and Kathy, wearing cool, pastel cottons, came downstairs. The boys wore light slacks and jackets.

Everyone gathered in the living room, attractive with its colorful draperies, rugs, pottery pieces, and rich, solid walnut furniture. A ruby-red glass containing iced, pink liquid was served to each guest. As they sipped it with enjoyment, Señora de Santis explained what the drink was.

"It is pomegranate juice," she said, "mixed with lemon and sugar."

"This is delicious," Kathy told her. "I've never heard of a pomegranate outside of my history books. The Greeks ate them, didn't they?"

"Yes. It is a pity the fruit is not popular in your country."

Just then, Linda spotted an ornate basket in a corner. Inside it were two tiny, bright-eyed, tan dogs. "How cunning!" she exclaimed. "What are their names?"

Señora de Santis informed her. "They're Chihuahuas, named Pepe and Tito."

Linda went closer. The little fellows jumped up on their embroidered red cushion and yipped furiously.

Linda laughed. "Small, but not timid!"

"Nobody would ever dare bother them," Bob commented.

Their hostess smiled. "The Chihuahuas are pretty belligerent creatures until they get to know you. Then they are very affectionate." She went over, picked up both dogs in her hands, and cuddled them under her chin. "Their fierceness to strangers is Nature's way of helping them survive despite their small size."

Kathy giggled. "If you're tiny, you make a big noise. If you're huge, you jut out your chin. How about us in-betweeners?"

"You just use your brain," Bob said with a grin.

"I'll try," Kathy said, laughing.

The group wandered out onto the patio to sit down until dinner was ready. They had been there only five minutes when suddenly Linda noticed Rango lift his head and cock one ear. He gave a low, rumbling growl and stared at some high, dense plantings of hibiscus beyond the house.

"Probably one of the *vaqueros* passing by," Señora de Santis explained.

Linda did not comment. A sudden fear had swept over her that someone who did not work at Quinta Floresta might be spying on the family to keep track of where they were. An enemy, perhaps!

Apparently Bob had the same suspicion, because he arose quietly and sidled toward the plantings. Rango followed. A moment later the two made a dash among the bushes.

By this time, those on the patio could hear swiftly running feet and the dog barking excitedly. Then came pounding hoofbeats.

"Someone is riding away!" cried Linda.

"And fast!" Larry exclaimed.

Everyone ran toward the hibiscus. By now, Bob and Rango had pushed their way through the bushes and joined the others.

"Señor de Santis," said Bob, "I think a man was hiding here listening to our conversation. You all probably heard him ride off."

Linda nodded. "Can you describe him?"

"I didn't get a very good look at him, but he's tall and slender, with a large mustache. He was on a rangy, fast-moving Morgan."

"He does not sound familiar. He doesn't work here," the ranch owner said, frowning. "I wonder why he was eavesdropping."

The subject of a spy in connection with the mystery of the vanished stream was not mentioned by Señor de Santis, so the Craigs did not refer to it. Linda and Bob, however, exchanged significant glances with each other and with Kathy and Larry.

A maid came to announce dinner, and they went into the softly lighted dining room, with its carved, brass-studded, mahogany furniture. The tablecloth was hand-embroidered, the Mexican silver tableware attractive with its cactus motif.

Linda's eyes lighted on a bowl of mammoth, pitted green olives which stood on the table. Their centers were filled with red pimientos and pickled white jicama root.

When they were passed to Linda, she looked at the olives and thought, We *must* find the water to keep the trees alive!

The welcoming meal was elaborate, and was served by two young Mexican girls. Each course was recognized by the four Americans, but the preparation of the dishes was new to them. The turkey had been cut into pieces, fried brown, and baked in a hot pepper sauce. Spicy vegetables were served in small, individual dishes. Sweet potatoes had been cooked with pineapple, and the mixed green salad was marinated with *salsa*. Dessert was a delicious pudding of shredded fresh coconut.

Linda thought, This is wonderful, but I'm stuffed!

Talk turned to the mystery, and Bob asked Señor de Santis, "You have determined that Agua Vieja did not turn down into an underground channel?"

The hacienda owner nodded. "Yes. At least, nowhere that is visible. The source is in a rugged rock mountain, and of course we do not know what happened there. The engineers I engaged could not give the answer. They seemed to conclude that the trouble had been caused by some freak of nature, an earthquake probably. But I found out that no tremors were recorded on the government seismograph."

"We've been wondering," said Linda, "since the disappearance of the water was apparently not caused by nature, it might have been planned by someone wanting to cause you harm."

"Even put you out of the olive market," Bob added.

"I'm afraid so." Señor looked around gravely at his visitors. "But I have no known enemies."

"And how could anyone divert a stream without its being seen?" Larry asked.

"That is the crux of the mystery," their host said. He smiled appealingly. "You young people with your fresh ideas and spirit gladden my heart. Let us hope that you can arrive at a solution."

"We've going to try very hard to do that," Linda assured him.

Señora de Santis smiled at her guests. "But also, you must have a good time while you are here. We have planned several interesting trips."

"And we must do some practicing for the big Fiesta de Cortés, in which we're scheduled to ride," Linda said.

"Ah yes," Señor de Santis responded. "That is the big fiesta to commemorate the arrival in Mexico of Hernando Cortés in 1519. He had with him a troop of more than six hundred men and ten cannons. Also he brought along sixteen thoroughbred Spanish horses to start a fine equine strain in Mexico again. Thousands of years before, there had been horses in America, but they had about died out. Why, we don't know."

"That's fascinating," said Linda, always intrigued

by the history of any place or event, and especially if horses were involved.

Just before going upstairs to retire, the Craigs proposed a before-breakfast ride.

"Fine with me," Larry said, and Kathy agreed.

Early the next morning, at Señor de Santis's suggestion, the Old Sol group rode out to a hard, flat half-acre to one side of the hacienda. When they started to exercise the horses, they found the animals skittish and wild after their long day of standing in the trailers. The riders could accomplish little more than get the knots out of the horses' backs and the jumpiness out of their systems.

Linda patted Chica d'Oro. "You'll be all right in a little while, baby. We'll ride some more after breakfast." She knew that, once the horses' gaits were smoothed out, these well-trained mounts would be a dependable lot again. Two hours later the Californians were in the saddle once more.

Señor de Santis joined them, astride a sleek, chestnut Spanish barb. Linda rode up to him, eagerly asking, "Are you ready now to lead us along the streambed?"

"Yes, indeed," he replied. "I know you want to get started on our mystery."

They rode at a canter, with Rango running alongside. Then the group walked their horses single file, with Señor de Santis leading the way through the many groves of beautiful olive trees. The irrigation ditches were dry, and in many places the ground had begun to crack.

When they reached the silty rock bed of Agua Vieja, Linda said sadly to Bob, "This is tragic, really tragic."

"You're so right," Bob agreed as the five began to scrutinize the dry streambed, hoping to pick up some kind of helpful clue.

Linda kept her eyes glued to the ground. The horses had covered two miles without the young sleuths' obtaining a single lead, when Linda stopped and dismounted. Quickly she picked up a torn scrap of paper from the ground. On it was scribbled the word "Ensenada." She showed it to the others.

"Is it somebody's name or a town?" Kathy asked.

"The resort town of Ensenada isn't far from here," Linda remarked. "This could be a clue."

The searchers went on. Linda trotted Chica to one side along the former streambed. Suddenly, the filly's right hoof buckled, and the palomino went down on her knee.

At the same moment Linda was catapulted over the horse's head!

A Puzzling Offer   4

"Oh!" Kathy screamed as Linda landed with a thud on the dry ground.

Linda had learned early in her riding lessons how to take a spill without being caught under a fallen horse. Therefore, she had pulled in her head, crossed her arms tightly across her chest, and rolled away like a cocoon in case Chica might go down on her side.

The other riders dismounted and surrounded Linda. Rango touched her with his nose, giving small, whining barks.

"Say something!" Kathy gasped.

Linda slowly got to her feet. "I'm—I'm okay. "How's Chica?"

Señor de Santis turned to the palomino, who was

favoring her right front hoof with an easy pawing in the silt. He ran his fingers down the pastern and examined the frog.

"Is there a sprain?" Linda asked worriedly.

"No injury," he answered. "And her shoes are all right. I think her hoof must have skidded on something."

Linda took the reins and led Chica in a small circle. The horse did not limp.

"Well," Kathy exclaimed to Linda, "you should apply for a job as an astronaut to the moon! That's how fast you went over Chica's head."

Linda laughed, then began to hunt for the object on which the palomino had skidded. Suddenly, her sharp eyes detected a metal object. She picked it up.

"A horseshoe!" she cried out.

The others quickly joined her, and Señor de Santis studied the shoe closely. Bob asked, "Could it have been thrown by one of the ranch horses?"

The owner shook his head slowly. "I do not believe so. This shoe has an L-shaped imprint not used by our blacksmith."

"Do you suppose," Linda said, "that the person who dropped the paper scrap was riding along here? And maybe he was the mysterious eavesdropper at the house?"

"It seems a logical deduction." Señor de Santis kept the horseshoe, and the searchers went on. They finally stopped to stare up at a sudden, steep rise of the mountain, formed almost entirely of boulders.

Linda turned to Señor de Santis. "I believe the answer to the missing water lies buried up there someplace," she said, pointing.

"The engineers have investigated the mountain," the rancher told her, "but found no explanation."

Kathy stared at the towering rock formation. "Just how, I'd like to know, are we going to poke around up there to find out anything?"

"That's right," said Larry. "No wonder the engineers couldn't figure out what happened to Agua Vieja."

"Engineers usually go by set theories and instruments," Bob remarked. "*We* must look for the unusual."

His sister pointed toward the southern slope, which was a mass of boulders. "Then I think we should explore up there," she said.

Señor de Santis spoke up. "Even if you figure it out, I'm afraid you'll have to climb up on another trip. We must return to the ranch for lunch. Directly afterward, I have an appointment at a fish cannery I own on the coast."

The riders returned to the ranch, where lunch awaited them on one of the wide porticoes. The Chihuahuas were playing nearby. Rango discovered them, and stood looking at the tiny, hairless animals with uncertainty.

"He doesn't believe they're dogs." Kathy laughed.

Rango turned away disdainfully. One of the Mexican serving girls brought Rango a pan of water and another of boiled fish. The latter was a new food for Rango. Hungry though he was, he sniffed it dubiously. Against his better judgment, he took a small bite and reacted with pleased surprise. He began devouring the fish greedily.

Bob grinned. "Safety first, eh, old fellow?"

Luncheon for the ranchers and their guests consisted of eggs fixed with black beans, Mexican rice, and cold milk. As they ate, Linda mentioned the paper she had picked up with the word "Ensenada" on it. "If neither that nor the horseshoe was dropped by anyone from Floresta," she said, "I'd like to find out who the person is."

Señor de Santis responded with interest. "You feel that there is some connection with our mystery here?"

"Yes," Linda admitted.

"In that case," the ranch owner went on, "perhaps you'd like to go with me this afternoon. My cannery is near Ensenada. You could do some sleuthing in town."

The visitors were receptive to the idea. Linda said, "We'd love to. We'll take the horseshoe along. Who knows—we may pick up a clue."

"You think you'll find the lost water in the

Pacific?" Larry said, teasing her. "And the villain swimming in it?"

Señora de Santis smiled, then said, "Something to know and remember about Ensenada is that it's said to be the place Robert Louis Stevenson wrote about in *Treasure Island*. He was inspired by the colorful history of pirates and the treasure-laden ships from the Orient sailing into lovely, blue Santos Bay."

"Let's hurry and dress for the trip," Linda urged.

When they came back to the portico, ready to leave, they found Señora de Santis pacing back and forth. "I am so distressed!" she cried. "Pepe has disappeared!"

Linda ran over and peered into the dog basket. Only Tito's bright, little eyes met hers.

"Could Pepe have crawled out by himself?" Bob asked.

"I suppose he might have," their hostess said, "but he's not used to running around alone. We always take the dogs on leashes for their exercise. I'm afraid something has happened to Pepe!"

"We'll look for him," Kathy volunteered.

The boys joined in the search and ran out onto the lawn to examine the bushes and shrubs around the edge of it.

Linda sidled up to Bob. She looked worried. "You don't suppose Rango—" She paused, reluctant to voice her fears.

Her brother grinned. "I know what you mean.

Rango didn't seem to be overly fond of the little beasts, but I don't think he'd dognap one!"

Linda sighed. "I hope you're right. It would be horrible if he caused any trouble when he wasn't even expected to come here with us."

"Don't worry, Sis," Bob counseled. "I'm sure Rango has nothing to do with Pepe's disappearance."

The four young people thoroughly searched the grounds near the house, but found no trace of the little Chihuahua. Then, suddenly, they heard barking in the distance.

"Rango!" Linda cried, and began to run toward the sound.

"He's in the olive grove," Bob said.

Kathy and Larry followed the Craigs at a fast pace until they reached the grove of grayish-green trees.

"Rango! Rango!" Linda called.

The barking continued. It seemed to come from inside the grove a little to the left. The young people plunged on.

"There he is!" Kathy called.

Rango was standing at the edge of an irrigation ditch, barking madly. As the Old Solers watched, he stretched his neck down into the ditch. The next moment he raised his head, the little Chihuahua held firmly in his mouth!

Linda ran forward and took the tiny animal from the dog. "He was saving Pepe!" she cried proudly. "And here I was being suspicious of him! Pepe probably wandered down here and fell into the ditch."

"And Rango followed and pulled him out!" Bob continued. "Good dog!" He patted the shepherd's big, yellow head.

When Señora de Santis saw Linda coming back to the house carrying her pet, she smiled happily. Then, hearing the tale of Rango's rescue, she bent over and hugged the big dog. "You are a real hero!" she cried.

When Pepe was restored to his basket, Señora de Santis said that her husband had decided to go ahead and hoped the young people did not mind taking one of their own cars. Bob drove his to the ranch-house entrance. Linda had just opened the car door when Rango bounded up beside her and planted two paws inside.

Larry laughed. "He's not going to miss out on this trip!"

Linda puckered her forehead. "He could go with us if I had a leash. Not expecting Rango to stow away, I didn't bring one," she told her hostess.

"We have had big dogs here," Señora de Santis said, "so there are several leashes in the house." She called to one of the serving girls. "María, bring the strongest leash you can find from the utility room."

When it was handed to Linda, she snapped it on Rango's collar. He gave a joyful bark and jumped into the car. As Bob drove along the sunny countryside, he remarked about the horse-drawn wagons on the road and the plows in the fields being pulled by horses.

"I like this," Linda murmured. "It's so quiet and peaceful."

"Primitive, though," Larry said. "There's not a bit of farm machinery in sight, and the little adobe huts look as if their occupants aren't at all prosperous."

"But happy, I'll bet," Kathy declared.

Bob slackened his speed. He grinned. "The slow pace of these people is contagious!"

"That's fine," said Kathy. "Let's not rush!"

In a little while, Bob parked the car at the edge of Ensenada, and they walked into town, with Rango pulling on the leash. The streets were lined with fascinating handicraft shops, many of them under protective shades made of maguey matting supported by tall poles. There were simple and elaborate restaurants, and small and large hotels. A dark-skinned family group sat on the pavement in front of one hotel, making baskets.

"Look over there!" said Linda.

In a small, open-front cubicle, a plump, smiling woman was frying peanuts in a mixture of olive oil, garlic, and little hot peppers. She held out a bagful to the passersby. Kathy took one. When she put a coin into the outstretched hand, the woman burst into a torrent of *gracias*.

"What did I do?" Kathy asked.

"Probably you overpaid her," Bob said.

"Well, good for me." Kathy grinned. "And I don't even want the peanuts!"

Linda then inquired of the grateful woman if there were any blacksmiths in town.

"I know of one," was the answer. "He lives not far from here."

She gave directions, and the Old Solers had little trouble locating the man's adobe dwelling with a small shed attached. The blacksmith proved to be friendly and smiled at his visitors.

Bob held out the horseshoe. "Do you remember forging this—or one similar to it?"

The Mexican was prompt in his reply. "No, I would recognize any shoe I make. This is not one."

"Do you know any other blacksmith who might use this mark?"

"No, señor."

Disappointed, the four callers thanked him and turned away. "No progress so far," Larry remarked.

Linda, never discouraged for long, pointed to a long, shaded bench near a water fountain and suggested, "Let's sit down awhile and watch the people go by. We might see someone who could help us."

"It would be just like my sister," said Bob, "to find the Agua Vieja villains right here!"

Linda chuckled. "I wish I could."

She took in the captivating scene intently. Little,

barefooted children, with shining faces and dressed in white cotton suits, played about. They kept their bright eyes on the tourists, apparently hoping that a coin would be tossed their way. Nearly all the men wore strawhats of some sort, from work-battered field types to elaborate sombreros.

Most of the girls and women had on colorful skirts and low-necked, white blouses. They wore dark shawls either over their heads and shoulders or made into a sling for carrying a baby on the hip.

"Is that a *rebozo?*" Larry asked.

"*Sí, sí,*" said Linda cheerfully.

The foursome went through some of the better shops, admiring the fine, wood carvings and unique turquoise, gold, and silver jewelry. A couple of fashion shops carried the hand-embroidered men's shirts. "Shall I buy one for each of you boys?" Kathy teased.

"How about it Larry?" Bob asked. "Think the fellows at college would go for them?"

"I don't know," Larry replied. "But I could go for a cold drink right now!"

"Me, too!" Kathy chimed in.

The four young people walked along until they came to a sidewalk café. They found a table at the edge and ordered limeades.

Linda looked up to see a little boy at her elbow. He wore ragged clothes, his dark hair was too long, and his face was dirty. But he had large, brown eyes and an appealing smile. He held out an American twenty-five-cent piece.

"You give me pesos for this, lady?" he asked. "Man in market no take American money."

"He probably can't spend American silver here," Bob agreed. "Have you some pesos, Linda?"

She took our her purse and put some pesos into the little boy's hand. A look of incredulity spread over his face.

"*Gracias, señorita!*" he cried. He turned and ran down the street.

"Well, you certainly made his day happy, Linda!" Kathy commented as they turned to their limeades.

For a few minutes, they discussed the mystery of Agua Vieja. Then Larry looked down the street. "Uh-oh," he said with a grin. "Look what's coming!"

Six little boys were running toward them. When the youngsters reached the café, they clustered around Linda. Each one held an American coin— some had nickels, some dimes, and some quarters.

"You give us pesos, lady?" they all asked eagerly.

Linda threw up her hands in mock horror. "Wait a minute!" she cried. "You'll break my bank!"

The little boys giggled, but continued to look at her beseechingly.

"Okay," Linda said with a smile. "I'll give you pesos, but don't bring any more of your friends. Understand?"

Six little heads nodded vehemently.

"*Muchas gracias!*" they sang out as they took the coins Linda gave them. Then they turned and raced into a nearby bakery.

Linda had fastened Rango's leash to a pole. He lay quietly but kept his eyes on the passersby. A few minutes after the children had left, a short, thickset, cotton-garbed *peón* with sandaled feet and an old straw sombrero came along leading a large, tan-colored dog.

Rango immediately jumped up in friendly greeting. The other dog was responsive, and the two circled each other in a playful caper. The *peón* stood and watched with delighted interest for a few moments, then looked over and asked the Old Sol four, "He your dog?"

"Yes, he is," Bob replied.

"Fine dog. Yes, very good dog. Fine big neck." Now the *peón*, talking to himself, repeated, "Good, big neck." He looked at the visitors and said, "You will sell the dog to me, yes?"

"Oh no," Linda replied quickly. "We will not sell him."

The *peón* regarded her solemnly for a few moments. Apparently deciding that he could not bargain with her, he tugged at his own dog and they went on. Rango sat down with his tongue hanging out the side of his mouth, looking longingly after them.

Linda puckered her forehead. "Why do you suppose that man mentioned Rango's big neck?"

"Down here, it may be considered a mark of good breeding," Larry offered.

Presently the four young people strolled out toward their car. Not far away they saw the *peón* and his dog again. He was talking to a tall, slender man with thick, black hair, who wore tight-fitting clothes and carried an elaborately embroidered jacket over one arm.

Rango immediately leaped forward to greet his new friend. In the few seconds it took Linda to pull him back, she noted the unusual design of the embroidery on the man's jacket. It looked like a modernistic bull decorated with gardenias. Linda wondered excitedly if the owner was a matador.

The two men had stopped talking, and now looked at the Old Sol quartet intently. Then they turned and walked away, the peasant pulling along his reluctant dog.

"I think that other man is a matador," Linda said. "Did you see his jacket?"

Bob nodded. "What strikes *me* is, those two are an incongruous pair."

"Which means, I suppose," said Kathy, giggling, "that they are plotting some sinister move."

The Old Solers reached the car, and Bob headed it for Quinta Floresta. When they were within sight of the hacienda buildings, the four were startled to see wisps of smoke.

"The stables are on fire!" Larry cried out.

"Oh, Chica!" gasped Linda fearfully. "Chica!"

Grim-faced, Bob bore down heavily on the car's accelerator.

The Invisible Speaker 5

The fire appeared to be coming only from the roofs of the Quinta Floresta stables, but as the four companions drove closer, they saw smoke billowing from the stalls as well.

Bob pulled up, and the young people jumped out and dashed into the building to get their horses.

Chica d'Oro was standing against the back wall trembling with fright. Half-choking from the smoke, Linda grabbed the filly by the mane and attempted to tug her toward the door.

"Come out, baby! Quick! Chica, come on! You must come!"

The palomino stood as if rooted to the stall, panic in her big, brown eyes.

The smoke was becoming thicker. "Chica, please!" Linda begged, tugging harder. "Come, or we'll both suffocate!"

She saw that the horse was frozen with terror. Desperate, Linda slipped off her sweater and wrapped it over Chica's head, blindfolding her. Next, she snatched off her skirt belt and tightened it around the palomino's neck.

Coughing and holding a handkerchief over her own nose and mouth, Linda got the filly moving toward the door. Quickly she led the palomino outside and took her across the yard under a jacaranda tree. Linda saw that the boys, too, had had to blindfold their horses to get them out, Larry with a gunnysack, Bob with his shirt.

"Kathy!" cried Linda. "Where are Kathy and Patches?"

Both boys raced back to the stables and plunged into Patches' stall. Larry came out leading the horse blindfolded with his shirt. Bob was carrying Kathy. He put her down beside Linda.

Kathy started to cough. "I—I'll be all right— soon as I get some of this fresh air. Wh—where is everybody? Nobody's fighting the fire."

"I'll guess we'll have to do it," said Linda.

Quickly the boys tied all the horses to jacaranda trees, and also Rango, who was excitedly getting underfoot.

Then Bob said, "Larry and I will climb onto the

roof. You girls hand up buckets of water to us. I saw several empty ones standing on the other side of the barn."

As the girls ran to fill the buckets, the boys got a ladder and clambered up. It was precarious standing on the roof of charred, smoking timbers.

Linda and Kathy raced back and forth from the well and scooted up the ladder with the buckets. Finally the fire fighters had the blaze under control enough to keep it from spreading farther.

By this time, two *vaqueros* who had been working on the far side of the ranch rode in. They had seen the smoke from a distance and stopped at the house for more buckets and a couple of hoses. It was not long before the group had put out the fire completely.

Señor de Santis drove in a few minutes later. His lips were white and his eyes sad as he stared in dismay at the charred roof. He thanked the young people for their quick work.

"I'm glad you got your horses out," he said. "How did the fire start?"

"We don't know," Bob answered.

One of the *vaqueros* spoke up. "I believe it did not happen by accident. It must have been set by a person who knew no one was watching from the house. My wife and the maids are probably taking their siestas. The firebug also knew that we *vaqueros* had gone over to the other side of the ranch."

Señor de Santis shook his head, mystified. Then

he straightened up with dignity. "I cannot understand this. If anyone picks up a clue to the fire, let me know. There are four empty stalls in the barn across from this one where I keep my horse. Put yours in them."

He looked sternly at his men. "One of you be on guard here at all times. Tomorrow I shall bring fire extinguishers for the stables. With our limited supply of water, we will have to be doubly cautious."

Chica d'Oro, meantime, was fretting at her tie rope, pawing, and giving short, broken whinnies.

"Chica's very nervous," Linda said. "I'd like to take her for a canter along the beach before putting her in a new stall."

"You will have time before dinner," said Señor de Santis. "We will not eat until eight o'clock. My wife is with a friend and will not return until then."

"I'll go with you, Linda," Kathy said. "Patches and I need some breezy salt air to clear the smoke from our lungs."

Bob said quietly to his sister, "I think Larry and I had better stay with Señor de Santis."

She nodded. "Keep an eye on Rango, will you?"

The girls hurriedly changed into jeans and saddled their fussing horses. They rode from the ranch along a back road to the white beach that was just beyond Quinta Floresta's western boundary.

Linda and Kathy cantered a short distance down the smooth, hard sand, wheeled, and cantered back. Then they stopped to let the horses blow.

"Oh, this feels good!" Kathy exclaimed, her fair hair flying back from her face, and a pink tinge in her cheeks.

"It's a real tonic," Linda said. "Look! All Chica's nervousness has vanished."

The girls sat dreamily looking out over the blue water of the bay. Their eyes were attracted to an old fisherman who stood nearby casting for perch in the surf.

"Look at those birds!" Kathy cried, and indicated a myriad of gulls flying overhead. "They go up and down without flapping their wings. They must be radar-controlled."

The old fisherman turned around, a smile on his face and his black eyes twinkling. "Gulls go on currents of air, *señorita*."

Kathy gazed at him thoughtfully. "But why wouldn't that make them go down when they want to go up?"

The fisherman laughed and explained in Spanish, "Gulls have the instinct to know where rising currents of air are most likely to be, and how to find them. A soaring gull can head into a column of air, and by gliding around within the column, can continue to go upward."

"That's fascinating," said Linda. "Sea gulls are smarter than I realized."

The fisherman continued, "If conditions are right, the gulls will dare to soar out to sea. Otherwise, they stay safely on the beach or float on the water." He assumed an amused expression. "Gulls don't have to telephone the weather bureau for the air temperature or wind direction and velocity. They know it themselves!"

The girls laughed heartily, and Linda commented, "There are times when I wish I had the instincts of a gull."

"And some wings," Kathy added.

She and Linda waved good-bye to the friendly fisherman, then took a couple more short canters along the beach.

"We'd better start back," said Linda finally. "We've come a good distance."

They rode at a leisurely pace in the direction of the ranch. On the way Linda suddenly spotted a stocky man racing across a Quinta Floresta field. With him was a large, tan dog.

"Isn't that the same *peón* and dog we saw today in town?" she asked excitedly.

Kathy shaded her eyes against the brilliance of the setting sun. "I'm not sure, at this distance," she said. "Especially with that big sombrero he's wearing. But if so, I wonder what he's doing around here."

Instantly Linda recalled the man's interest in Rango; also how he and the matador had stared at the Old Solers.

"Let's find out!" she exclaimed, and galloped off in the stranger's direction.

Kathy tried to keep up with her pal, but the palomino, with her fast-paced Arabian ancestry, was too fleet for Patches. In a few minutes, Linda disappeared into a grove of cypress trees.

By the time Kathy reached it, her friend was not in sight. "Linda! Where are you?" she called.

When no answer came, Kathy felt panicky. Had Linda fallen and been injured? Had the strange dog attacked her?

"Linda!" she screamed.

Then, to her relief, a voice called back, "Coming!"

Linda appeared, looking crestfallen. "I lost sight of that man," she said. "I'm sure he was up to no good, because when he saw me, he ran off like a deer."

"I'm glad he did," Kathy answered. "We mustn't forget what Bronco told us—that we're in a strange land and must be careful."

Linda said nothing. Secretly she wished that they had overtaken the *peón* and been able to question him.

Back at Quinta Floresta once more, Linda noticed that Rango was tied to a tree near the barn. After she had taken care of Chica, Linda pulled the dog's blanket bed into the palomino's stall. Then she untied Rango and brought him a pan of food from the kitchen. She knew that as soon as he finished eating, he would have a run and then settle down for the night with his equine pal.

After dinner the de Santises and their guests gathered on the patio. Señor de Santis's face reflected his deep concern over the stable fire.

Even his lighthearted wife was markedly upset. "I just cannot imagine who would do such a dreadful thing," she said.

"Maybe it's the person who tampered with your water supply," Bob proposed.

Enrique de Santis was startled at this suggestion. "I did not think of that. I do know I am in serious trouble about the water," he said. "I spoke with a neighbor before dinner to see if I might share his water supply, but the expense of piping it to Quinta Floresta is too great. And now comes this danger of an arsonist sneaking in here."

Larry spoke up. "I just can't believe anyone would kill fine horses on purpose. Perhaps the fire was not started deliberately, but was an accident."

"Yes, that is possible," Señora de Santis quickly agreed.

"But," said Bob, "if the fire *was* set, maybe it was for another reason—an attempt to hurt our horses enough to keep them out of the Fiesta de Cortés."

Linda gasped. "Oh, Bob, how wicked!"

"We will see that nothing happens to your valuable horses," the ranch owner said determinedly. "I shall have *vaqueros* on guard night and day to make sure."

"Oh, thank you, Señor de Santis." Linda smiled gratefully.

His wife changed the serious aspect of the conversation by saying, "I am afraid we have forgotten that you young people also came here to have fun. Is there anything special you would like to do tomorrow?"

"I'd like to take another ride up Agua Vieja," Linda replied, "and investigate those rocks. That will be fun for me—working on the mystery."

"I'm for that," Larry said. "We'll have to start early to beat the heat."

"Right," Bob agreed.

"You must take food and water if you plan to spend some time up there," their hostess said. "I'll have lunches put up and ready to pack in your saddlebags."

"*Gracias!* That's very kind of you," Linda told her. Just as the Mexicans and their guests were about to leave the patio, Linda recalled the strange *peón* the girls had seen crossing the ranch field. She told the story and the others showed surprise.

Linda asked, "Señor de Santis, could he be a neighbor? He is a short, heavyset man, and his dog is about the size of Rango. We are sure we saw them in Ensenada." She related the rest of the encounter in town.

The rancher thought for a moment before replying. "No, I haven't any neighbor who fits that description."

"Well," said Linda, not wishing to bring further worries to the de Santises, "I guess it *was* a coincidence—the man was just hiking with his dog." But she had an uncomfortable feeling that he had not been on Floresta land by chance, and that he had some sinister purpose in mind.

By sunrise next morning, the Old Sol group had their horses saddled, their lunches packed in the leather bags, and the canteens filled.

"Where do you suppose Rango is?" Linda asked suddenly, missing the big, yellow dog.

Bob gave a few sharp whistles, but Rango did not appear. "Don't worry about him," he said with a grin. "You know how Rango has to be doing something all the time. He's probably down on the beach chasing those gulls you were telling us about."

The group finally rode off, and after a pleasant, uneventful ride arrived at the awesome mountain of rocks. They worked their way around to a section where they saw that it would be possible to climb a distance on foot. The ascent was not so steep here, and there were level spots among the big boulders. After tethering the horses, they took their provisions and started upward.

"I just know there's a plausible explanation for the disappearance of Agua Vieja," Linda insisted as she carefully skirted a boulder.

"It may be plausible," said Bob, "but it's sure elusive."

Before long, Kathy suggested that they stop to rest and eat. She chose a fairly level plot of ground, and everyone sat down.

"I've never been in such a still place," Kathy said in a hushed voice when they had finished their lunch. "Somebody say something."

"Not me," said Bob. "I was about to take a snooze—that is, if I can find room to stretch!"

They sat in silence for a while, enjoying the peaceful atmosphere. Then suddenly, out of nowhere, a man's sharp voice broke the stillness.

"It's working top-notch," he said in Spanish. "Great idea of yours, Little Barco."

The young people exchanged startled glances. Without a word, they jumped up and began searching about the rocks for the speaker. There was no one in sight. *Where* could the mysterious voice have come from?

Rango Vanishes 6

"We *did* hear a voice, didn't we?" Kathy finally broke the silence.

"We certainly did," Linda said firmly. "Since no one is in sight, the voice must have come from somewhere among these rocks!" She continued to search through the boulders for a few minutes without finding anyone.

Suddenly Linda straightened up with a laugh. "Larry Spencer," she said accusingly, "were you pulling a ventriloquist act on us? You used to be good at throwing your voice."

Larry grinned. "Not guilty this time!" he protested.

Bob looked thoughtful. "Rocks and mountains sometimes deflect sound waves. Maybe that voice we heard was an echo of words spoken some distance from here."

"Anyway," said Linda, "Let's all try to remember the voice in case we hear it again."

"I wonder what Mr. Voice looks like," Kathy mused.

"Probably he's a tall, dark, handsome Mexican," Larry replied teasingly. "Remember he spoke in Spanish!"

"In that case we must find him!" Kathy said quickly.

Linda laughed, then grew serious. "He may have had something to do with the disappearance of the water. For that reason alone, I'd like to find him."

Bob agreed that the mysterious voice might well belong to a man involved with the dried-up stream. "But we seem to be stymied at the moment. It's getting very hot. I suggest we start back to the ranch."

The two couples slid down the rocky mountainside to their dozing horses. They cinched up their saddles, exchanged tie ropes for bridles, which had been left swinging from the pommels, and mounted.

"Let's ride home on the other side of the stream," Linda proposed. "Perhaps we can spot that 'Little Barco.'"

They turned their horses through the matted, weedy ground cover. Though the grass was tall in some spots, it bent easily under the horses' hooves. There was no one in sight.

Linda was sorry. I wish we could have found the person whose voice we heard, she thought. At least he might have given us some helpful information.

The riders made their way slowly, enjoying the gentle breeze. As they rounded a curve, Bob suddenly exclaimed, "Look at those buzzards!"

A half-dozen of the large, black birds were circling in the blue sky. The riders were close enough to see the black, leathery skin of their heads and featherless necks.

Kathy shivered. "Ugh! They're horrible things! There must be something dead over there."

"It isn't dead yet," Bob told her, "or the buzzards wouldn't still be circling. Let's go over and see, Larry. It may be some stock we can help. You girls stay here."

As the boys rode off, Linda observed, "I agree that buzzards are repulsive, but they do keep the countryside cleaned up."

In the meantime, Bob and Larry had arrived at the gap. Searching for the cause of the buzzards' interest, they saw an old, gaunt, maverick cow go down on her knees and topple over.

The boys jumped off their horses. "Come on!" Larry cried. "Maybe we can get her up and scare those scavengers away!"

Bob shook his head. "We can't do anything. She's gone."

As the boys sadly turned back toward their horses, the flock of buzzards descended with a great flapping of their large wings. But instead of going for the cow, they dived at Bob and Larry!

"Hey, get away from us! We weren't trying to steal your food!" Bob cried. He and Larry covered their faces with their arms in an attempt to escape from the vicious beaks.

Linda and Kathy had ridden through the gap. When they saw the buzzards attacking the boys, the two began to scream at the top of their lungs. The girls rode as close as they dared and stood in their stirrups, waving their big hats.

This diversion made the fierce birds rise into the air for a few moments. It was long enough, however, to enable Bob and Larry to jump into their saddles and gallop away from the cow.

"Let's get out of here!" Bob urged.

As the four riders spurred their horses back through the gap, Larry panted, "That's the last time I'll ever try to interfere with buzzards!"

"You boys are hurt!" Kathy cried, noticing streaks of blood on their hands.

"At least they didn't get our handsome faces!" Bob joked.

Linda suggested that antiseptic should be put on the scratches. "We'd better take the shortest way home," she added.

When the group rode up to the stables, the

vaqueros insisted on taking care of the horses. For once, the riders agreed and hurried into the house.

Señora de Santis exclaimed in distress when she saw the boys' wounds. She quickly applied antiseptic and adhesive bandages.

"Perhaps you would like to go and freshen up," she said. "*Merienda* will be served in the portico when you're ready."

"What's *merienda?*" Kathy whispered to Linda on the way to their rooms.

Linda laughed. "That's the name of Mexico's traditional hour for hot chocolate and cakes."

"Sounds good to me!" Kathy grinned.

As soon as Linda had bathed and put on fresh clothes, she ran outside to call Rango. The frisky, yellow dog did not answer her summons.

Linda caught sight of Señora de Santis in the shady portico. She was feeding tidbits to Prevenido, the cockatoo.

"Do you know where Rango is?" Linda asked.

Señora de Santis turned. "Why, no, he hasn't been around all day. I thought he was with you."

"I couldn't find him this morning when we left," Linda said in a worried tone.

At that moment, the others came out. "Rango's still not around," Linda told them unhappily. "I'm worried. He hasn't been seen since last night. We must look for him!"

"Don't worry about Rango, Sis," Bob said comfortingly. "You know how he goes off on expeditions of his own at home. He's probably doing the same thing here."

"But he may have been stolen!" Linda cried. She was thinking again of the *peón* who had wanted to buy Rango, and of the mysterious man who had been near the hacienda.

"I'll bet old Rango has found a dog friend," Larry declared, "and they're playing together. He'll come back when he gets hungry."

Linda was still unconvinced, and voiced her fears. "I'm afraid that man who spoke of Rango having a big neck may have stolen him."

"Why, Linda," said Kathy, "no one could hold Rango if he didn't want to stay. Any dog who can fool the border guards and run into Mexico is able to take care of himself!"

"Sure," said Bob. "As a matter of fact, it's even possible Rango was picked up by an inspector and is being held at the border."

"That could be," Señora de Santis agreed. "Why don't you telephone and find out?"

Linda put in the call. She learned that no dog was in captivity at the station.

When she reported this to the others, Señora de Santis laid a sympathetic hand on Linda's. "Rango will return soon, I'm sure. Now let us talk of the Fiesta de Cortés tomorrow. We are all eagerly looking forward to seeing you and your golden horse perform."

Linda gasped. "That's right! The fiesta *is* tomorrow." She turned to her friends. "In the morning, we must have a practice session on our precision foursome."

Before Linda went to bed that night, she slipped out to talk to Chica. The palomino stood with her head over the door looking doleful. She glanced back of her at Rango's vacant horse-blanket bed.

Linda went into the stall and hugged the filly. "Rango will come back," she whispered in the horse's ear. Chica nickered and bobbed her head up and down as if in agreement.

"I hope we're right," Linda added wistfully. "Tomorrow we must think only of riding our best. Will you do that?"

Again Chica nickered and bobbed her head.

"You're such a comfort to me," Linda said. She gave her pet one last hug and went into the house. She continued to worry, not only about Rango, but about the barn fire as well. The same man might have set the fire and then taken Rango.

Despite her worries, Linda forced herself to sleep well to be alert for the fiesta performance. She and her friends were out early the next morning. Everyone from the main house and the bunkhouse gathered to watch the drill in a small circular corral—Señor and Señora de Santis, the servants, and the *vaqueros*. The horses were in fine condition and pranced about as if eager to begin.

At a signal from Linda, the riders, who stood in a

line, put their mounts around the ring in the walk, trot, and canter. Then they reversed in perfect precision. Next, maintaining the canter, they went into their drill. They broke in twos, changed to a single line, each going around the other, then formed in twos again, and finally back to fours. Each horse was on the right lead in each formation. It was a beautiful demonstration of precision riding.

The spectators clapped and shouted, "*Olé, olé!*"

While Kathy and the boys pulled their horses to the side of the ring, Linda walked Chica slowly around the circle to calm her down and put her in the mood for her own special performance.

"Steady, baby," she coaxed.

In a few minutes, Linda guided Chica around the corral in the four-mile parade gait, then the five-mile. The palomino picked up her dainty hooves to exactly the right height and with just the correct showiness.

The *vaqueros* gave cheering shouts of approval. As Señor de Santis helped Linda dismount, he said enthusiastically, "I've seen many fine parade horses, but never one to equal your Chica!"

"I'm sure you'll win all the prizes today," Señora de Santis assured her guests with a smile.

"We'll be happy if we can bring back just one," Linda replied.

The four young people washed and groomed their horses until they shone. Then they loaded the animals into the trailers and hurried to the house to change their clothes. In a short time, they were ready.

Since Señor and Señora de Santis planned to have lunch and watch the show with friends, they drove their own car to the fiesta grounds. The Old Solers followed in their cars with the horse trailers.

As they neared the fiesta site, Linda gave an exclamation of excited delight. A colorful scene lay ahead.

The show spot was a permanent one. Tall shade trees and blooming bushes surrounded the arena's high, yellow adobe wall, which was ornamented with fancy, mosaic tile designs. Tall standards with fluttering multicolored banners rose from the top at every few feet.

A sign directed the show participants to a shady lot in back of the arena.

After parking their cars and trailers, the Old Sol foursome hurried into the grounds, where, besides the horse show arena, they saw many booths of refreshments and games.

"Let's try our luck," Bob urged.

Eagerly they played some of the games of chance. They threw balls and hoops, and tried to shoot out candle flames with water pistols. But none of the group won a prize.

"I guess this just isn't our day," Linda said finally with a rueful laugh.

Kathy was busy tossing small hoops over the neck of a bottle. Three hoops on the bottle meant winning the game. Twice she had managed to circle two.

"Come on," Bob said, "we'd better eat and get back to the horses. The Grand Entry is at one o'clock."

"I can't leave now!" Kathy wailed. "I think I've discovered the secret. It's all done with a flip of the wrist."

A crowd had stopped to watch. Kathy held the ring before her for a second. Then she sent it flying toward the target. She did this three times, and each ring dropped neatly over the bottle neck.

The crowd laughed and cheered. The black-mustached concessionaire beamingly handed her a beautiful straw basket. "Your prize, *señorita!*" he said.

"*Gracias,*" she answered. "Well," added Kathy with a laugh. "I have one prize at least to show for the day!"

The four ate a quick lunch at a nearby food booth, and hurried back to the trailers to get ready for the performance. They looked with pride at their horse equipment, purchased just before leaving California. The matched outfits consisted of stainless steel bits, headstalls ornamented with stainless steel spots, and carved leather, Cheyenne roll saddles decorated with steel conchas and spots.

Linda and Kathy had made four bright, aqua, felt saddle blankets edged with white wool fringe. The four friends had also invested in matching suits of aqua gabardine and shirts trimmed with white leather fringe. Boots, hats, and gloves were white.

"If I do say so," commented Kathy, "we look right sharp!"

Although the Grand Entry was replete with gorgeous Spanish, *charro*, and Arabian costumes, the Old Sol riders drew enthusiastic applause as they passed the grandstand, four abreast.

The equestrian competitive events in the fiesta horse show, besides the single-rider classes, were for groups of four, six, and eight. Linda was the only one of the Old Sol riders who had entered an event alone. This was the Parade Horse Class.

The foursome made up the first scheduled event. In addition to the Old Sol quartet there were a *charro-charra* class, a family, an all-boy group, and an all-girl group. A blue ribbon and trophy would be awarded to the first-place winners and ribbons down to fifth place.

The ringmaster instructed all five groups to ride around the ring at the same time in the walk, trot, canter, and reverse. Then each unit put on its individual performance.

The Old Sol contestants went through their drill with perfect precision. The *charros* were dramatic, the family unusual and appealing. The foursomes of boys and girls put on simple but expert performances.

"Come in and line up," the ringmaster called over the loudspeaker.

The competitors complied. Upon noticing the judge still bent over his card, tallying his points, Linda and Kathy exchanged tense glances. At last, the judge handed his decision to the ringmaster, who carried it to the announcer.

The crowd was hushed as he read off the awards, starting with the fifth-place, pink ribbon. The family group received this. Then the white ribbon was awarded to the girls, the yellow to the boys, and the red to the *charros*.

Finally, with a fanfare roll of drums, the thrilled Old Solers were presented with the trophy and four blue rosettes! Linda, who had been designated by the other three to accept the award, put Chica into a bow of thanks.

The grandstanders went wild. The band played and cameras clicked as Linda, radiant, rode up to accept the trophy. It was a magnificent replica of the gate to the fiesta grounds, mounted on a mahogany platform. Across the top was a strip engraved with the words FIESTA DE CORTÉS. In the center was a golden equestrian statue of Hernando Cortés, and below this the engraved gold plaque of the winning class.

Linda cantered from the ring, holding the trophy high in one hand. Outside the boys quickly changed Chica's gear to her silver outfit while Kathy helped Linda change into her green embroidered and jeweled suit for the Parade Horse Class.

"Good luck, *amiga*," Kathy whispered, and Bob and Larry gave Linda reassuring grins.

When everything was ready, Linda took Chica away from the other horses and walked her back and forth along a row of trees. Gradually the palomino's excitement from the quadrille riding subsided. "That's the baby," Linda said. "Calm and steady." Then she mounted and rode over to join the other contestants.

It was an open class of eleven—six men and five women—riding the most beautiful horses Linda had ever seen in a single class. She was particularly impressed by an Appaloosa, black save for a spotted rump and white mane and tail. Its rider was a very pretty young Mexican girl in a rose-colored suit. Linda smiled at her and received a shy smile in return.

When the class finally filed into the arena, the Mexican girl was near the front, while Linda rode toward the end. Working around the ring, Linda watched the girl with a strange feeling. The Appaloosa had almost the same gait and action as Chica, and the Mexican girl rode like Linda. They might have been twins!

A handsome young Mexican on a tall, chestnut saddle-bred passed Linda twice. He seemed to be a favorite of the crowd, which cheered him enthusiastically.

Finally the call came to ride in and line up. There

was an impatient buzzing from the stands. The judge seemed to be taking an unusually long time to arrive at the final results.

Linda sat outwardly composed, but with her heart pounding rapidly. A great hush of suspense fell over the arena as the judge finally passed his decision sheet to the ringmaster. The crowd was absolutely silent as he handed it to the announcer. The man gripped the microphone and began to read the list.

Sea Project 7

Linda swallowed nervously as, one by one, the ribbons were given out. She knew that from the class of eleven, only five could be awarded ribbons, and she looked curiously at the other contestants. All appeared calm and confident.

Four ribbons had been given out. Only the one for first place remained. Linda's name had not yet been called.

Perhaps I didn't even place in the first five! she thought sadly.

Linda realized that the names of the girl in the rose-colored suit and the man on the chestnut horse also had not been called. One of them must be the winner of the blue ribbon!

As the announcer hesitated, the ringmaster and

the judge stepped over to his table. The three held a short conference, while the people in the stands stirred restlessly.

Then the announcer took up the microphone again. "There is a tie for first place," he said. The crowd once more was silent.

It must be between the girl and the good-looking man, Linda told herself. I think the girl is the better rider.

The announcer cleared his throat and continued, "The winners are Señorita Concha Ríos, riding Rey Hermoso, and Señorita Linda Craig, riding Chica d'Oro!"

There was a storm of applause as the two girls urged their horses up to the stand. Although elated, Linda felt every nerve tingle. How would the tie be resolved?

The member of the Mexican Council who had donated the trophy stood next to the ringmaster holding the prize. It was a beautiful shaft of onyx and gold, two feet tall.

After the applause had died down, the announcer went on, "Our judge, Señor Agustín, feels that these riders are too evenly matched for a runoff. Therefore, we have decided that the awarding of the prize will be determined by the toss of a peso."

A murmur of dissent rose from the grandstand. Linda glanced at Concha. The Mexican girl's face was downcast and her big, brown eyes were filled with tears of disappointment.

Immediately Linda came to a decision. She rode up to the judge's stand and said a few words to the ringmaster. With a smile, he nodded and handed her the microphone.

Linda drew a deep breath and said tremulously in Spanish, "Riding in this Parade Horse Class has been one of the most thrilling experiences in my life. To have been chosen one of the winners has made me very happy. However, I do not feel that this trophy should leave your beautiful country. I therefore request that it be presented to Señorita Concha Ríos."

The crowd roared, applauded, and whistled their approval. With tears, now of happiness, streaming down her face, the Mexican girl rode up and accepted the trophy and the blue ribbon. Then she and Linda cantered from the ring side by side.

When they were outside the arena, Concha rode close to Linda. She leaned over and put her arm around the American girl's shoulders. *"Gracias,"* she said softly. *"Muchas gracias.* That was a lovely thing to do!"

Then she held out the long-streamered blue rosette. "This I want you to have—for a memento from me. You have earned it."

Linda smiled happily. "All right," she said. "I'll treasure it always. And now, good-bye until we meet again."

"Hasta la vista," said Concha.

The two girls waved to each other and rode in

opposite directions. Back at the trailer, Kathy and the boys were waiting to congratulate Linda.

"You were wonderful, honey!" Kathy cried as she threw her arms around her friend.

Bob grinned widely. "Nice going, Sis! I'm proud to be your brother!"

"Great stuff!" exclaimed Larry.

At this moment, Señor and Señora de Santis came up to add their praise.

The rancher beamed, and his wife said, "We are very proud of you. I am thinking that the magnanimous young *Americana* on the golden horse will be remembered for a long time in this part of Mexico."

Many strangers stopped to congratulate Linda and her friends on their fine horsemanship. Bubbling over with their success, the group started for home. It was dusk when Linda and Bob drove into the Quinta Floresta stable yard.

Linda jumped out. "Rango, Rango!" she called. "Come here! I want to tell you something."

At this moment, one of the *vaqueros* appeared. "The big dog, he not come back," the man said sadly. "I look for him, but no good."

"Oh dear!" Linda sighed. "I did so hope he would be here. It would be a perfect ending to a beautiful day!"

"He'll return. I'm sure he will," Bob said with forced cheerfulness.

Linda was not to be distracted. "Rango may need help this time. I'm not going to sit back and wait!"

she said spiritedly, and hurried up to the house.

Señor de Santis was standing on the patio. "How do I call the police?" Linda asked him. "I'm positive Rango has been stolen."

Her host nodded. "I have begun to think that myself," he said. "But may I suggest we wait until morning? If Rango is not back by that time, I'm sure the police will start a search for him."

Linda was forced to be content with this. But she secretly resolved to drive around the area herself the next day and make inquiries for the big dog.

The following morning, when the family and their guests were eating an early breakfast in the portico, Linda suddenly gasped. "Look! Rango!" The big shepherd was limping toward them. He came over to Linda and collapsed at her feet.

"Oh, Rango!" the worried girl cried.

She pushed back her chair and dropped to her knees beside the exhausted dog as the others crowded around. Tenderly she ran her hands over him, searching for injuries. She found none.

Rango hung his big tongue out one side of his mouth, and rolled his large, eloquent eyes at her. He seemed to be saying, "Oh, if I could only tell you what happened to me!"

"You poor, poor dear," Linda murmured. She told the others, "His throat chain is gone. A bigger collar was put around his neck—I can tell by the way his hair is matted down. And his pads are sore. I think he has walked a long, long distance."

"But from where?" Kathy asked.

"And why," said Larry, "would anyone put a different collar on him?"

"To try to prove new ownership, I suppose," Kathy replied. "Of course it didn't do any good— Rango must have slipped out of it and run off."

Linda was thinking hard. "You remember that man in Ensenada who talked about Rango's big neck and wanted to buy him. Do you think there could be any connection between him and our dog's disappearance? He stole him because he couldn't buy him?"

Bob said practically, "What puzzles me is, why would the man go to so much trouble? Rango is a grand dog for us, but he isn't worth a tremendous amount to sell."

The group continued to speculate, and finally Señor de Santis said that he would notify the police to be on the lookout for anyone who might be a dognapper.

"And I'll alert the department about the mysterious *peón* you mentioned."

Rango was fast asleep, but awoke as Linda finished eating. He stood up, looked at the food remaining on the table, then placed a paw on Linda's lap. The dog gazed appealingly at her.

"That's as plain an order for breakfast as any I've ever seen," Señor de Santis said with a laugh.

His wife rang the bell for María, a serving girl. When the maid came out and saw Rango, she clapped her hands in delight. "The lion dog, he come back! I am glad!"

"Bring our unexpected guest some meat, biscuits, and gravy," Señor de Santis instructed her. "Also a bowl of fresh water."

When the meal arrived with more meat than biscuits, it was evident that the happy María had prepared it herself. Rango ate hungrily, then lapped up the water in the bowl.

Though grateful and relieved at the dog's return, Linda was disturbed. She resolved to protect him.

"He mustn't be enticed away again," she said determinedly.

"I suggest," she said to the others, "that we work some more on the mystery of the vanished stream." She turned to Señor de Santis. "Do you think the water could have changed course and be flowing out of the rocks some distance from the mountain?"

"It's possible," he replied. "However, the engineers investigated this and found no such indication."

"I'd still like to continue exploring that rock mountain," Linda said thoughtfully. "I can't forget the strange voice we heard."

"Okay," Kathy agreed. "When do we start?"

"Please, not for another day," Señora de Santis said with a smile.

The young people looked at her with surprised interest, waiting for an explanation.

Their hostess went on, "You must not forget that

the Youth Exchange visitors' program requires a certain amount of sight-seeing. I understand you must submit reports when you get home."

"Yes, we must," Linda answered.

"Then," Señora de Santis continued, "I will tell you of a trip my husband has planned for you today." Her eyes danced, indicating that something special was in store for the Old Solers.

"I hope you are all good sailors," her husband said mysteriously.

"You mean we're going out on the ocean?" Kathy asked, amazed.

Señor de Santis smiled. "Yes. We will drive down the coast about fifty miles to see the fish cannery belonging to a friend of mine, then take his speedboat to the island of Guadalupe. There you can watch the sea elephants."

"Sea elephants?" Larry repeated. "I've noticed sea lions at the zoo—they look like seals with ears. Are sea elephants similar?"

"No, they are quite different, you will learn." Señor de Santis grinned broadly. "I think they will be a big surprise to you."

"We will leave as soon as you are ready," his wife said. "After the trip, we will go to Ensenada and have dinner at the Rosita Hotel. They have a picture gallery there with the works of some of Mexico's finest artists on display. I am sure you will enjoy looking at the paintings."

"We will!" Linda said enthusiastically.

"Linda likes to sketch," Kathy told their hosts. "She has had several of her desert paintings on exhibit."

"I should like to see them," Señora de Santis said with interest.

"Kathy is exaggerating," Linda protested. "But I hope you will visit us someday and I will show them to you."

She then looked at Rango with renewed concern. The big, yellow dog was stretched out on the floor, sound asleep.

"Is there someplace inside the house where we can keep him while we're gone?" she asked. "I don't think he'll mind for one day, and I'll have a much better time knowing he's safe."

"Of course," Señora de Santis replied. "The utility room should do. You boys might take a pad from one of the outside couches for Rango to lie on."

Bob and Larry got the pad and led Rango across the portico into the utility room. With a weary sigh, the dog dropped onto the bed and immediately fell asleep again.

Within an hour, the Quinta Floresta party was speeding south along a secondary beach road. The ocean beyond sparkled under the bright morning sun, as waves swelled, gathered speed, and broke on the shore.

The cannery they came to was a long, low

building near the water in a cove. Beside it was a private wharf with several fishing boats moored to it.

"We'll visit the cannery first," Señor de Santis said. "My friend isn't here, so I'll show you around myself."

He led the way into a room where workers were busy boning a huge pile of fish. As they finished each fish, it was lifted onto a narrow moving table and carried to a machine where it was cut into pieces. These went through more machines, which placed the chunks in cans and sealed them. Now they were ready for sterilization.

"These fish were caught this morning," Señor de Santis told his guests.

Kathy whispered to Linda, "I hope they taste better than they smell!" She wrinkled her nose.

"I guess one gets used to that," Linda replied. "These workers don't seem to mind it."

Nevertheless, both girls took great gulps of fresh air when their host led them from the cannery onto the dock. The fishing boats tied up there were sturdy forty-footers with cabin and mess aft.

Señor de Santis pointed to the open space in the bow of a nearby boat. "They fill that with ice," he explained, "and the catch is kept there until it can be brought into the cannery."

"Sitting on ice today might be a good idea in this heat," Kathy observed with a grin.

Señora de Santis laughed. "I'm sorry to disappoint you, Kathy, but we must go in that." She pointed toward a colorful speedboat named the *Angela.* A green- and yellow-striped awning shaded the stern, which was furnished with comfortable lounge chairs and a small, round table.

"Pretty neat!" Bob remarked.

They went aboard. As soon as the group was seated, Señor de Santis took the wheel, and the jet-propelled boat set off at a good clip. It soon left the cove and headed into the Pacific.

Larry stretched out in his chair, both arms above his head. "This is great," he said, "especially after so much traveling by horseback and car."

For the next three hours, the young people enjoyed the brisk sea air and dazzling sunshine, then lunch was served amid stories and jokes from everyone.

Later Bob suddenly sat up straight. "Land ho!" he called, pointing to a high, rocky island straight ahead.

"That is Guadalupe," Señor de Santis said. "Keep your eyes open!"

The young people hurried to the rail and peered interestedly at the land mass. The next moment they heard an ear-shattering cry. It seemed to issue from the ocean directly in front of them!

"What is that?" Linda exclaimed in alarm.

Strange Matador 8

As Linda asked the question, the sound came
again—a bloodcurdling bellow. Everyone turned to
Señor de Santis for an explanation of the frightening
noise. His eyes were twinkling and his lips twitched
with amusement, but he did not reply.

Suddenly the answer came to Linda. "The sea
elephants!" she gasped.

"You have guessed it," he said.

"But we must be a mile away from the island!"
Larry exclaimed.

"That's right," Señora de Santis agreed. "The
creatures' cries can be heard a great distance.
They are tremendous animals with a great lung
capacity."

"They certain are," her husband declared. "Many of the males weigh several tons. The females are smaller and, I might add, a little less ugly."

The weird roars grew louder as the *Angela* approached the island. Its skipper anchored as close to the rocks as he dared, and the visitors lined up along the rail.

"These sea elephants look more like seals than elephants," Larry remarked. Their heads, with rolls of creased hide where a neck might be, were tufted and whiskered.

"Ugh!" Kathy made a face. "I've never seen anything less attractive," she declared.

Linda giggled. "In a beauty contest, how would you ever make a choice?"

The enormous mammals sprawled on the rocks, their color hardly distinguishable from the gray of the stone. Except for raising their heads to give an occasional roar, the sea elephants were almost motionless.

Larry ran from spot to spot, taking pictures. Bob grinned. "You planning to give me an enlargement for my room at college?"

Larry retorted, "It might scare you into studying."

Linda stared at the sight ahead. "What do the sea elephants find to eat on those rocks? They must consume a lot to grow so big."

"The ocean floor all around this island is covered

with an abundance of sea life and growth," Señor de Santis explained. "They don't have to move far or work hard to find plenty of food."

One huge elephant at the edge of the rocks appeared to be disturbed by the bobbing craft. He rolled his head from side to side, and his thick hide quivered. A smaller elephant next to him, evidently his mate, moved a flipper languidly.

Suddenly, the male gave a loud roar and slipped off the rock into the water. His heavy bulk caused a tremendous wave that rocked the de Santis boat dangerously.

"He's coming toward us!" Kathy cried out. They could see the great bulk moving swiftly in their direction.

"Enrique!" Señora de Santis cried. "We'll be capsized!"

Her husband barked out an order to the boys to raise the anchor. He started the motor, thinking this would scare off the beast.

But the sea elephant was not discouraged. With amazing speed for his huge size, he cut through the water toward the boat. The *Angela* began to move.

"He's gaining on us!" Bob cried.

In an effort to get out of the path of the oncoming animal, Señor de Santis made a sudden turn. The boat tilted precariously. Kathy, who had been leaning far over the rail watching in fascination, suddenly lost her balance and was thrown overboard. The next second she was floundering in the water!

"Oh, Kathy!" cried Linda, looking aghast at the fast-approaching sea elephant.

Quickly Bob seized a life preserver that was fastened to the rail and tossed it overboard. "Grab this, Kathy!" he yelled, and prepared to jump in after her if necessary.

Kathy bobbed up and shook the wet hair from her eyes. "I'm okay," she called. "Just pull me in! *Hurry!*"

The skipper maneuvered the boat so that it was between the girl and the onrushing sea mammal. Kathy clung to the buoyant ring, and Bob and Larry hauled her aboard.

"Oh, thanks," she said, panting and dropping to the deck, as the *Angela* sped away.

"That was a weird time to choose for a swim," Larry said, teasing her. "Were you planning to race the sea elephant?"

Kathy gave him a scathing look as she tried to wring the water from her full, cotton skirt. The elephant, apparently deciding that he had vanquished his enemy, turned and swam toward shore.

"I never want to see one of those creatures again!" Kathy sighed in relief.

"Come below, my dear," said Señora de Santis. "I'll give you something to wear while your clothes are drying."

A few minutes later, Kathy came up on deck in an attractive bathing suit and short, flowered coat.

As they all seated themselves in the deck chairs, Linda remarked, "I'm glad you got pictures of the sea elephants, Larry. We can use the prints to illustrate our reports to the exchange people. These creatures have to be seen to be believed."

"Too bad we can't add their sound to our reports," Larry remarked.

They had been so busy with the sea elephant episode that they had not looked over the water. Now Bob said, "There's another boat." He pointed to a small motor launch some distance away, but apparently following their wake. Two men were in it.

"They may be fishing," Señor de Santis remarked. "It is a very popular sport in this area."

"One of the men is standing up," Linda observed as the other craft drew a little closer. "He's looking at us through binoculars!"

"Maybe he's a member of the shore patrol," Larry said, adding jokingly, "He's checking to see if we've stolen a sea elephant!"

Linda was taking the matter seriously. She got up, walked to the rail, and peered intently across the water. "That man standing up looks familiar," she said in a puzzled tone. "He's tall, slender, is wearing tight-fitting clothes, and has a shock of black hair. In fact," she remarked excitedly, "he resembles the man who was talking to the *peón* with the big dog that time when we were in Ensenada."

"The matador?" Kathy asked.

"Yes."

As if he realized that he had been observed, the man sat down in the launch, and it sped toward shore.

"Why was he staring at us—as if he were spying?" Kathy wondered uneasily.

No one had an answer, although Linda was sure that the man's interest in them boded trouble. Señor de Santis had cruised among the islands for a while, then turned back to the mainland. By docking time, Kathy had put on her dried clothes. Then they got into the car and headed for Ensenada to have a late dinner.

When they arrived at the Rosita Hotel, Bob suggested that Señor de Santis go in with his wife and let him park the car.

"That's very kind of you," their hostess said with a smile. "The parking lot *is* a good distance behind the building."

"We three will go along to keep you company, Bob," said Linda as the car pulled up in front of the hotel entrance.

"We'll meet you in the lobby," said Señor de Santis as he and his wife alighted.

Bob parked, and the young people started up a side street toward the hotel.

Suddenly Linda took Bob's arm and whispered, "See that tall man coming toward us? I think he's the same one who was watching us today from a boat, but he has changed to looser clothing."

"And he does look like the fellow we saw in town," Bob agreed. "Let's see if he recognizes us."

The four spread out until they took up practically the entire sidewalk. But to their surprise, the man paid no attention to them. He merely stepped around the group and went into a nearby food shop.

"Well," Kathy exclaimed, "he certainly didn't act as if he'd ever seen us before!"

She and her companions had paused in front of the food store. Now they heard men's voices inside. One asked, "What has become of Little Barco? I haven't seen him today."

"Barco—Little Barco!" Linda whispered excitedly. "That's the name mentioned by the mysterious voice in the mountain! Wait here!"

Linda walked into the shop and looked around. The proprietor, an elderly Mexican wearing a big, white apron, stood behind the counter. He was wrapping a package for the man who had just entered.

When the storekeeper saw the girl, he spoke up hastily, "*Sí, señorita*. You wish—"

Linda made a quick decision. "Pardon me," she said, "I am looking for a person by the name of

Barco. Little Barco, he is called. Can you tell me where I might find him?"

The two men exchanged startled glances. The black-haired man shook his head, while the proprietor shrugged and said, "I know of no Little Barco." He handed the parcel to his customer.

Linda became suspicious immediately. She had noticed the look that had passed between the men. She was sure that they knew Barco but for some reason did not intend to let her know this.

She thought, I'm certain now that Barco is mixed up with these men, and they all know at least part of the reason why Agua Vieja has disappeared. Instead of being put off, Linda determined to try to find out something further. She stepped up to the tall Mexican.

"The other day I saw you carrying an embroidered jacket. The pattern is most unusual. Does the design of the bull and gardenia have some special significance?"

Again a startled look flashed across the man's face. "You are mistaken, *señorita*," he said somewhat brusquely. "I have no such jacket. I wish you good day and Godspeed." With that, he bowed and hurried from the shop.

Discouraged and puzzled, Linda followed. The man's nervousness and reluctance to talk convinced her that he was not telling the truth. Why had he denied owning the jacket? What was there about it to startle him when she had mentioned it? Could the jacket be a secret signal of some sort?

By the time Linda reached the sidewalk, the man had crossed the street and was getting into a car parked at the curb. She dashed after him.

"What's up?" Larry called, following her.

"A clue, maybe."

Linda was just in time to read the license as his car pulled away from the curb. Quickly she took a note pad from her purse and jotted down the number.

"Tell us what you're doing," Bob demanded when the group was together again.

Linda's voice was excited. "I think we have our first real lead in the Agua Vieja mystery. Let's hurry to the hotel. I want Señor de Santis to make a phone call for me."

The couple was waiting in the lobby, as promised. "May I ask a favor of you, Señor de Santis?" Linda asked immediately. "It's in connection with the mystery."

"Why, of course," the rancher said with keen interest. "It will be my pleasure."

Linda told him of their latest encounter and of hearing Little Barco's name mentioned in the store.

"I believe the shopkeeper was asking the man we saw in the boat about him," Linda went on. "The tall man denied having the jacket when I asked him about it, and rushed outside. But I have his license number."

"Clever!" Señor de Santis said approvingly. "And now you want me to—"

"We must learn who he is," Linda said eagerly, "and I thought perhaps the police could find out through the automobile license bureau."

"I shall call immediately," Señor de Santis declared. "That might be very valuable information." He excused himself and walked briskly toward the telephone booth.

While waiting for him, the others went to look at the hotel's paintings. The exhibit had been set up in a room directly off the lobby. Linda noticed that the series of colorful oils provided a picture tour through all of Mexico. She paused before one painting of a church. "That is the Chapel of the Kings in Cholula," Señora de Santis told her. "Cholula is called the City of Churches because there are so many. It is said that one might go to a different church there every day in the year."

The young Americans walked slowly past the paintings. There was one of the Pyramid of the Sun in the old Toltec city of Teotihuacán, near Mexico City, and another of the Shrine of Guadalupe.

"This shrine was built on the spot where the Indian Juan Diego claimed to have seen the Virgin Mary in 1531," Señora de Santis explained.

She also pointed out a view of the blue bay at

Acapulco, where Spanish galleons once unloaded rich cargoes of silks and spices from the Orient. "Acapulco is now our most popular seashore resort," she added.

"Look at these odd fishing nets!" Kathy exclaimed, peering closely at a fishing scene.

"Those are the butterfly nets of Lake Pátzcuaro," their hostess said. "That is the only place in the world where such nets are used."

"They're fascinating!" Linda remarked.

There were pictures of colorful market scenes and some engaging ones of little Mexican burros. The Craigs and their friends were so engrossed they were startled when Señor de Santis returned and summoned them to dinner. He said that the police would telephone him.

Almost an hour went by before the call came. Linda waited impatiently to hear the results of the inquiry as to the name of the car owner.

When their host returned, he was smiling. "I have the information," he reported. "The car belongs to Fernando Porfirio, a matador."

"You were right, Linda!" Kathy exclaimed. "You guessed his occupation the first time we saw him."

"I *must* try to talk to him again!" Linda declared emphatically. "I want to find out why he wouldn't admit owning that jacket."

"And I'd like to know why his *peón* friend was so interested in Rango's big neck," Bob added.

Señor de Santis caught the Craigs' enthusiasm. "I

think I know a way you can see the man again," he said.

"How?" Linda asked.

"There is a parade of matadors at Tijuana before the bullfights tomorrow. We'll go there!"

Runaway Bull 9

"Oh, thank you!" Linda cried, her dark eyes shining in anticipation. "The parade of the matadors must be exciting."

"It is indeed," Señora de Santis remarked. "I am sure you will all enjoy watching the men in their fancy dress."

After a delicious dinner, the ranchers and their friends drove back to Quinta Floresta. As Linda jumped from the car when it stopped at the front door, a long, plaintive howl came from the utility room.

"Poor Rango!" Linda exclaimed. "How lonesome he must have been all day!" She ran across the patio and opened the door to the room.

Rango bounded out. The dog was so happy to be

released from his confinement that he ran from one to the other of the young people, sniffing their hands and giving rapid, little barks of welcome.

Bob took the dog for a run around the grounds, then fed him and coaxed him back into the utility room. "It's too late to give you a bath, which you need after that long absence of yours," he told the dog, "but prepare yourself for one in the morning!"

At the word "bath" Rango put his tail between his legs and curled up in a corner. Bob chuckled and closed the door. Meanwhile, Linda had gone to feed Chica and give her a few affectionate pats.

Next morning the de Santises and their guests were halfway through breakfast when a big stock truck drove in. It stopped before the house and a young man jumped out.

Señora de Santis looked up. "It's Felipe! He's back from California!" she cried.

"Come in, Felipe!" the rancher urged.

Everyone greeted the *vaquero* warmly.

"Our Josefina and Pedro," Señora de Santis said eagerly. "Are they well? Are they enjoying themselves?"

Felipe grinned broadly. "They send you greetings, as do Señor and Señora Mallory. Your son and daughter are having much fun. Cactus Mac, he sees to that. He took them to a town of ghosts."

"Ghosts?" Señora de Santis repeated, puzzled. "What sort of town is that?"

The Old Solers laughed, and Linda said, "I think

he means Cactus took them to a Western ghost town."

"These ghost towns really have ghosts?" Señor de Santis also looked uncertain.

Linda explained that, in the days of the big gold and silver strikes in the western United States, mining towns had sprung up almost overnight. Then when the veins of ore ran out, the people would leave to try their luck somewhere else.

"The towns are very quaint," she declared. "Most of the old buildings are still standing, and it's fun to prowl around them and try to picture the town as it was in the old days."

"That sounds very interesting," Señora de Santis agreed.

"Your friends come often to Old Sol," Felipe said to the Craigs, "and take Josefina and Pedro for long horseback rides. They eat wagon woodchuck under the stars."

The Old Solers' eyes twinkled with amusement.

"I have never heard of such a dish," Señor de Santis said. "What is it?"

Linda smiled. "It's actually what we call a chuck-wagon feed," she said. "Food that the cowboys eat out on the range is called chuck. The wagon that carries the provisions and cooking kettles is called the chuck wagon. They probably had steaks, beans, slaw, garlic sourdough bread, and apple pie."

"Gracious!" Señora de Santis exclaimed. "I

should think our children would be getting fat!"

Felipe pulled a small envelope from his pocket and gave it to her. "Pedro sent this to you, *señora*. He washed it for you in a pan."

Señora de Santis opened the envelope and peered inside. Then she turned it upside down on the table. A few tiny, yellow particles fell out.

"Why—it looks like gold," the Mexican woman said in surprise. "Where did Pedro get this, and what is meant by washing it?"

Bob spoke up. "Cactus Mac probably took Pedro to a stream where gold nuggets can still be found. The method used to get the gold out of a stream is called panning. The sand of the creek is dipped up in a pan that has a fine sieve bottom. The dirt is washed out when the pan is shaken, leaving only any gold that is present. Sounds simple, but there's a knack to doing it."

"This is a real treasure, then," the woman said with a proud smile as she carefully slipped the tiny nuggets back into the envelope.

"I am pleased that my son and daughter are having an informative as well as an enjoyable visit," Señor de Santis observed approvingly. "We are very grateful to your grandmother and grandfather for entertaining them."

Then he turned to the *vaquero*. "I see you have brought a truckful of horses. How many did you purchase?"

"Six, *señor*. Six fine quarter horses. I bought four for you and two for myself." Felipe flashed a smile at his employer.

"So you think you are going to make some profit, do you?" Señor de Santis said teasingly.

"*Sí, señor.*"

"Where did you get the stock truck?"

"It belongs to my cousin in Los Angeles. He is coming down here and will pick it up later. I will keep one horse and sell the other to a rich *charro*." He grinned in anticipation of the profitable deal. "That Bronco has good horses."

"Bronco?" repeated the rancher. "I thought you were buying the horses from Señor Mallory."

Linda laughed. "Bronco is my grandfather's nickname. Everyone calls him that."

"I see." Señor de Santis chuckled, then said to Felipe, "We are leaving shortly for Tijuana to see the Parade of Matadors. Unless you are too tired after you put the horses up, I would like you to drive us in the ranch wagon. There will be a crowd in town, so it will help if you can take care of the car."

"*Sí, señor,*" Felipe said cheerfully. "I am not tired." He got back into the truck and drove to the stable yard.

When everyone was ready to leave, Bob took Rango into the utility room again. The dog was obviously unhappy and sat back on his haunches looking reproachfully at him.

"Sorry, old fellow," Bob said, "but we can't take a chance on your running away again." Rango's reply was a sharp bark as Bob shut the door.

In a short while, Felipe drove the large car to the front entrance, and the party set off for Tijuana. When they arrived, the town was packed with natives and tourists awaiting the colorful spectacle.

The street outside the Plaza de Toros, the bull-ring, had been roped off for the parading matadors. It was hoped by the officials that the procession would persuade many onlookers to attend the bull-fight.

"Here come the matadors!" Kathy cried, clapping her hands in excitement.

Filing from the bullring was a line of fifteen matadors. Each wore the traditional black hat and black slippers. Their tight trousers ended just below the knee. Their bright-colored outfits were lavishly trimmed with gold and silver embroidery.

As the first matador passed the group, Kathy exclaimed in amazement. "Why, he has his hair in a knot at the nape of his neck!"

Señor de Santis explained, "That is the traditional *coleta*. The knot used to be the man's own, but now false ones are worn."

"They sure do strut!" Larry commented with a grin as the bullfighters marched past, shoulders back and hips thrust forward.

"That is the matador walk," Señora de Santis told him, smiling.

Linda had been staring closely at each man as he passed them. "I'm afraid Porfirio isn't here!" she said in disappointment when most of the matadors had gone by.

"There he is!" Bob whispered as the last man in line came into view.

"And he's wearing the strange jacket!" Linda exclaimed. "The one with the bull and gardenia design. Why did he say he didn't own it?"

Bob frowned. "Beats me."

The matadors paraded around the roped-off area several times while the spectators applauded. Then the bullfighters headed back into the ring.

"Let's try to talk to Porfirio now," Linda urged her brother.

"All right."

When Fernando Porfirio came opposite the Craigs, they fell in quickly beside him.

"I see you are wearing your bull and gardenia jacket," Linda said in Spanish. "Why did you tell me in the store yesterday that you didn't own one like this?"

The matador gave her a sharp look out of the corner of his eye. "I was in no store yesterday. I said nothing to you. I do not know you, nor what you are talking about."

Linda's heart sank. Evidently the matador insisted upon lying. But she decided to keep pace with the man and try again.

"You saw us in Ensenada the other day," she

persisted. "You had this jacket over your arm. You talked for several minutes to a *peón* who remarked that our dog Rango had a fine, big neck. What did he mean by that?"

At Linda's last question, the matador started nervously. "He meant nothing—nothing at all. Now, leave me alone!"

Bob had an inspiration. "Perhaps Little Barco can tell us what we want to know," he said.

An expression of alarm crossed Porfirio's face. He stopped and looked about in agitation. Suddenly he hailed two policemen who were standing near the entrance to the bullring. They ran over.

"Is something wrong?" one of them asked.

"These two Americans are bothering me with silly questions," the matador said to the officers. "I do not know them. Please get them away from me."

Immediately, one policeman took Linda's arm while the other grabbed Bob. A wave of laughter swept over the crowd as they saw the startled expressions on the young people's faces.

Linda flushed in chagrin and embarrassment. Then a disturbing idea struck her. Were she and Bob being taken to jail? She stopped abruptly and asked the policemen, "Where are you taking us?"

"We're going to lock you up for a while," one of the officers replied. "We can't have any troublemakers on the streets today."

Linda's eyes flashed angrily. "You must not believe what Fernando Porfirio said. He was lying."

"He *does* know you?" The officer looked surprised.

"Certainly," Linda said. "We have met him twice. My brother and I were only trying to get him to give truthful answers to our questions. We believe he is involved in a mystery we're working on."

The policemen exchanged glances. Then one of them said brusquely, "If there are any mysteries to be solved in Mexico, I advise you to leave them to the proper authorities."

"You two apparently did not cross the border just for the bullfights," the other officer stated.

"We're American Youth Exchange visitors," Linda replied. "We are here for three weeks as guests of Señor and Señora Enrique de Santis."

She looked around and saw their host and hostess, with Kathy and Larry, hurrying toward them. "Here come the de Santises now."

Upon hearing the name, a prominent one in the area, the police had released their holds on Linda and Bob. "Very well," one said quickly. "Remain with your friends. Do not attempt to talk to the matador again."

The two officers hastily returned to their posts at the bullring entrance.

"What did those officers say to you?" Señor de Santis asked indignantly.

Linda quickly explained the incident and Porfirio's actions.

Kathy was outraged. "The nerve of *him* calling the police."

"I thought you both were being dragged off to jail," Larry said.

"We were." Bob grimaced. "Linda talked them out of it."

"I apologize for our *policía*," Señor de Santis said. "With such crowds as this, however, I suppose they must be especially careful." Then he added, "Come, let us go into the arena."

"If you don't mind," Linda demurred, "I'd like to make some inquiries around here."

"I'll go with Linda," Kathy offered.

Señora de Santis smiled. "I had better stay with the girls," she said. "Linda may need extra help."

"Well, boys?" Señor de Santis looked at Bob and Larry.

"We're with you!" Bob answered, and the three hurried into the arena.

As the girls and their hostess turned and walked toward the business district, Señora de Santis asked Linda's plans.

"To make some inquiries. I'm sure Porfirio and Little Barco are in a plot together. Since Barco was somewhere on or near the mountain, he must have information about the disappearance of Agua Vieja. I must find him."

The three went into several shops. In each one, Linda asked the proprietor if he knew Little Barco or anything about him. No one did. Discouraged, the trio headed back toward the arena. They could hear excited shouts of *"Olé! Olé!"* coming from the spectators inside.

Just before Señora de Santis and the girls reached the street leading to the bullring, they saw a horse tied to a railing in front of a leather shop. The animal was a beautiful, liver-chestnut saddle-bred.

Linda ran up to pat him. "What a fine boy you are!" she murmured.

Suddenly there came terrified cries and screams from the crowd outside the Plaza de Toros.

"What's going on?" Kathy asked excitedly.

The three hurried up the street toward the plaza. There they saw a bull that had apparently escaped and was running around the outside wall of the ring. In another moment, he came thundering down the street. Terrified people were scattering in all directions.

"Quick, girls," Señora de Santis urged in alarm. "In here!" She and Kathy ran into a nearby bakery.

But Linda did not follow. She looked back at the tied-up saddle-bred. The angered bull was heading straight for him!

That horse will be gored! she thought in horror.

Quickly Linda made up her mind. She snatched the horse's tie loop, jumped onto his back, and turned the animal at a run down the nearest side street. The bull came plunging after her.

Linda made a sudden turn into a vacant lot,

hoping that the bull would continue straight ahead. But the enraged animal also veered. Snorting angrily, and with horns lowered, it charged directly at Linda!

Mountain Find　　　　　　10

Desperately Linda put her horse in a circle, hoping to wear out the bull, or at least to confuse it. The sleek saddle-bred had been well trained. It responded instantly to her knee pressure and the touch of the tie rope on its neck. The animal seemed to be aware of the menace bearing down on him from the rear.

Linda suddenly heard a new sound coming from behind her. The bull's snorting had stopped, and people were cheering. She whirled to see what had happened.

"Felipe!" she cried in surprise.

The *vaquero* had managed to throw his rope around the bull's heavy neck. Now he dug his heels into the dirt and sat down, hauling back on the lariat. The bull flopped over on its side and lay there, panting in exhaustion.

People poured from the shops and ran down the street. They were laughing and cheering. One excited Mexican cried, "This is a better show than the one going on in the ring!"

By this time, several handlers had pushed their way through the crowd. The bull was still worn out from his mad dash, and reluctantly allowed himself to be led back to the pens.

The throng surged around Felipe, clapping him on the back and calling him "Charro Felipe." Two of the men hoisted him to their shoulders. Ignoring the *vaquero*'s laughing protests, they carried him to the arena. Bob, Larry, and Señor de Santis stared in astonishment as the *vaquero* was paraded around to the wild acclaim of the audience.

Most of the crowd had followed Felipe and his friends. Meanwhile, Señora de Santis and Kathy hurried up to Linda, who had dismounted. "It was very brave of you to rescue this fine horse," her hostess said admiringly. "That was a dangerous bull."

"Felipe saved us both," Linda replied. "He is a wonderful *charro*."

"He shall be well rewarded, you can be sure," Señora de Santis declared, her voice trembling with relief that Linda was unharmed.

Linda thought of Felipe, disappearing on the shoulders of his friends, and the resounding cheers inside the arena. "I think he is being happily rewarded right now," she said, smiling.

Followed by Señora de Santis and Kathy, she led the chestnut back up the street to the railing. After she had secured his tie rope, she patted the strange horse. "It's been a pleasure to know you," she said softly. "You're a real honey!"

Kathy chuckled. "It's a good thing we decided to wear our full fiesta skirts today. You'd have had a time jumping on that horse in a tight skirt!"

Just then a middle-aged man hurried toward them from the direction of the bullring. He wore riding trousers and highly polished boots.

"My horse! My beautiful Viajante! He is all right? They said over the loudspeaker that the wild bull charged him and that a girl saved him." He looked around at the bystanders. "Where is this girl?"

"Right here," Kathy answered, and told the story.

The man looked admiringly at Linda. With a courtly bow, he swept off his big hat. "Señor Rincón, at your service. *Muchas gracias*, most beautiful American Linda. I speak for Viajante also. He is very grateful to be saved from a bad goring by your quick thinking. One moment!"

He hurried to the flower stand at the corner and returned in a few seconds carrying a large bouquet of creamy-white gardenias. With a flourish, he presented them to Linda. "Again, *muchas gracias, señorita.*"

"Thank you, Señor Rincón," Linda said. "The ride on your wonderful Viajante and this beautiful bouquet will be among my most cherished memories of Mexico."

She smiled, then on impulse asked, "Do you live in this part of the country?"

"*Sí, señorita,*" the man replied. "I was born and still live on a large ranch close by. I raise thoroughbred horses there."

"Have you ever heard of Little Barco?" Linda inquired.

Señor Rincón gave a wry laugh. "That one. Yes, I know him. Manuel Barco, the horse handler. A little, squat man, strong as an ox, although not liking honest labor too much. He worked for me at one time. But he was a wanderer. I do not know where he is now."

"I think he is working for Fernando Porfirio, the matador," Linda said. "At least I've seen him with a man matching that description."

Señor Rincón shook his head. "I would not think so. Porfirio does not own horses." Then he went on, "If you are thinking of hiring Barco, I would not recommend it."

He bowed again. "Now, if you will excuse me, I must get Viajante's trappings, which I left in this shop."

As he walked away, Kathy whispered to Linda, "Doesn't the name of his horse mean 'traveler' in Spanish?"

"Yes," Linda replied, "and he's well named."

Before the girls had a chance to discuss what they had learned about Barco, Señor de Santis and the boys ran up.

"Were you the girl who saved the horse, Sis?" Bob asked immediately.

When Linda nodded, Señor de Santis remarked, "You are a real heroine. You must tell us about it on our way home."

"I will. But first, tell me how you like the bullfights," Linda said as they walked toward the parking lot.

"Great," said Bob. "Those matadors sure put on a good show with their swirling capes."

"How was Porfirio?"

"He seemed nervous, and the crowd booed him," Larry told her.

Kathy laughed. "Linda upset him."

They found Felipe waiting at the car. He beamed when Linda thanked him for roping the bull. "It was nothing, *señorita*," he said modestly.

In the car once more and on the way to Quinta Floresta, Linda excitedly related her news. "I've found out more about Little Barco," she said. "His name is Manuel, and he's a horse handler. We'll probably find him working for some horse breeder." She gave a happy sigh. "I think we're really getting somewhere now."

Bob hugged his sister affectionately. "It's a nice

bit of information, but we want to hear about your rescue of that horse."

"Oh, beautiful Viajante! He would have been gored to death by that runaway bull," Linda explained. "I just jumped up on him and rode him off."

"With old *toro* snorting at her heels," Kathy added. "She put on quite an exhibition of tricky riding, trying to throw him off her track. She was doing pretty well, too. Then Felipe arrived and roped the critter."

Linda laughed. "And just in the nick of time." She buried her face in the fragrant gardenias. "Wasn't it sweet of Señor Rincón to give me these lovely flowers?"

"I know him," Señor de Santis said. "He is a fine gentleman. But you also did him a great service, Linda!"

"And you were quick to think of asking him about Little Barco after all that excitement," Larry commented.

"That's because the mystery is always on my mind," Linda explained modestly. "We *must* find out who or what caused the disappearance of Agua Vieja."

"That's right. When we get back to the ranch we should take our horses out for some exercise," Bob put in. The others agreed.

Linda's first act upon returning was to release

Rango from the utility room. He leaped joyously about, but would not come to Bob.

"He's mad at you for shutting him up," Kathy remarked with a laugh.

"Rango," said Bob, "can't you get through your dog brain that I did it for your own good? Do you want to be taken again by some dognapper and have to eat beans the rest of your life?"

Rango was not mollified, and when the riders started out he kept close to Chica's heels. Linda led the way toward the olive grove.

"I want to see how the trees look," she explained.

The young people found a group of ranch hands at work in the grove. They were busy cultivating the earth to provide aeration for the trees. Although there was some sign of wilt on them, they did not look too bad as yet.

Along the rows nearest the house, the workers were drilling deep, narrow holes about four feet from each tree. Into these, water from the well was being poured. In this way it reached the roots quickly.

"We can't go very far," said one of the men sadly. "The rest of the trees will die in a couple of weeks."

Linda said to her companions, "Let's start out early tomorrow morning on our horses and ride around the other side of that mysterious mountain."

"That's a good idea," Bob agreed. Kathy and Larry nodded.

At daybreak the following morning, when they

were ready to leave, Linda exclaimed with concern, "Rango's missing again!"

Bob called and they all hunted around the stable yard, but Rango was not found.

"I think he's hiding," Bob decided. "When we've gone off lately, I've shut him up. So he's not taking any chances this time!"

Linda brightened a little. "I suppose you're right. We'd better get started."

When they reached the rock mountain, Bob reined up. "I wonder what the best route is to attack this mass of boulders," he said.

"I suggest we start up the side where we heard the man's voice," Larry said. "We can go higher by a switchback trail."

"That sounds good," Linda agreed. "Then when we get near the top, we can make our way around to the other side of the mountain."

"To see what we can see!" Kathy chanted with a chuckle.

"Who knows what's on the other side?" Linda said with a note of excitement in her voice. "Perhaps we will find the answer to the mystery!"

The others caught her enthusiasm. "Okay," Bob cried. "Montaña Misteriosa, here we come! Lead on, Larry!"

His friend picked the trail with care. Single file, the four guided their horses in a zigzag course up the mountainside. It was hard going, with the horses slipping occasionally on the rocky surface.

Finally, about two-thirds of the way up, Larry came to a narrow shelf. He pulled Gypsy to a stop.

"How about it, gang?" he called back. "It looks as if we could ride around this to the other side. Shall we try it?"

"Oh, yes," Linda cried. "Let's!"

"I felt better going up than I will going around," Kathy remarked with a shiver as she glanced down the steep slope they had negotiated.

"Don't look down," Bob advised her. "Just focus your eyes between Patches' ears."

At that moment, a fly settled on one of the mare's ears, and she flicked them violently. Kathy giggled. "That's going to be a little hard to do!" she said.

Larry led the group slowly along the rocky shelf. Gradually, the trail grew less stony. Finally the riders rounded a corner. A broad, green valley stretched out far below them.

"How lovely!" Kathy cried.

"Isn't it?" Linda agreed. "They certainly have plenty of water down there."

"Probably from wells," Bob guessed.

"Let's investigate," Linda proposed eagerly.

The young people saw that the slope on this side of the mountain was less rocky. The soil was looser, and there were many gullies caused by erosion.

Larry surveyed the situation. "We'd better each make our own trail going down here," he declared. "Then if one horse slips, it won't start a chain reaction and land us all in a heap."

Following his suggestion, the riders spread out over the mountainside. Then each started a zigzag descent.

Kathy was between Larry and Linda. Suddenly, Patches slipped and began to slide down the slope on her hocks. Kathy screamed. The others reined up their horses and watched, paralyzed, as Kathy and Patches disappeared in a cloud of dust.

Bob held up a hand and shouted to Linda and Larry, "Don't move! You might start another slide!"

A few seconds later the dust subsided, indicating that the mare had stopped her descent.

"Wait here," Bob called, "until I see how things are." Carefully he made his way down the slope where Kathy and Patches had vanished. In a few minutes, he spotted them at the bottom of a deep hollow. Kathy was slumped over in her saddle with her head resting on the pommel.

"Come on," Bob shouted back to Linda and Larry, "but take it easy!"

When Linda reached Bob's side and saw Kathy, she called out in alarm, "Kathy, Kathy! Are you all right?"

The girl raised her arm in a little wave, but did not lift her head.

"What's the matter, Kathy?" Bob cried.

The girl sat up then, but she held a hand over her eyes. "My eyes are full of dirt," she called. "I can't see!"

"Hang on!" Bob shouted. "We'll get you out!"

"But how?" Linda gasped.

"What do you think, Larry?" Bob asked.

"Try to pull Kathy and Patches out on the lower side with a rope," Larry proposed.

The three made their way cautiously down the slope. They could see that the hole into which Kathy and Patches had fallen was lower on the far side. When they reached the pit, Bob pulled the rope from his saddle.

"I'll slide down and fasten this around Patches," he said. "You get on Rocket, Linda. Tie the ends of the rope to the pommel, and you and Larry pull Patches out when I give the signal."

Bob let himself into the hole and quickly made a firm rope harness around the pinto mare. At a wave of his hand, Linda and Larry spurred Rocket and Gypsy into action. At the same time, Bob slapped Patches hard on the rump to get her going.

Finally, with the horse's floundering leaps and Linda's and Larry's steady pulling, Patches and Kathy emerged from the hole. Larry untied the rope from the pinto and lowered it for Bob.

While he was scrambling upward, Linda soaked a handkerchief with water from her canteen and helped Kathy wash the dirt from her eyes.

"That feels better," Kathy observed shakily a minute later. "I thought I was blinded for life! And how about Patches?"

Quickly the boys examined the pinto and pronounced the little mare unhurt by her long slide.

Kathy insisted that she herself was all right, too.

"Then let's go on to the base," Linda suggested. "I'd like to ride around there and see what it looks like."

"Well, it certainly doesn't appear as if this side of the slope has had any water," Larry observed.

When they reached the bottom of the slope, the four riders went a short distance in both directions, but saw nothing unusual.

"We'd better ride around the base here until we strike rocky ground before we cross to the other side," Linda suggested.

"Rocks for me from now on," Kathy said with a little shudder.

Linda started on ahead. She had gone only a short distance when suddenly she reined up and called out. "Hold it! There's a cave-in here!"

She stood up in her stirrups and peered into the deep hole. Then she motioned excitedly for the others to come.

"See down there at the bottom!" cried Linda. "It looks like a section of a big pipe!"

The Mocking Laugh 11

Larry jumped off Gypsy. "I'm going down and take a better look at that pipe!"

At the same moment, Bob swung from his saddle and laid a restraining hand on his friend's shoulder. "Better not, Larry," he advised. "I'm afraid this soft earth might cave in on top of you and we wouldn't be able to get you out. We have no shovels."

"Bob's right," Linda agreed. "Don't take a chance. Let's try to figure out from this spot why that pipe's here."

"And not so close," Kathy muttered, cautiously backing Patches farther away from the cave-in.

"Okay," Larry conceded reluctantly. "But if I could just strike the pipe with something, I might be able to tell if it is still in use or has been abandoned." He looked around for a likely object to use.

"It could be an oil or gas line," Bob surmised.

"Or a water line," Linda added meaningfully.

"Where would the water come from?" Kathy asked.

Linda shrugged. "I wish I knew!"

Larry had not given up his idea of sounding the pipe. He picked up a rock. "I'm going to throw this down. Listen to the sound the pipe makes."

"I don't think you ought to," Linda objected. "It might break the pipe and we'd be destroying someone else's property. Also, gas or oil might escape."

"Well, we ought to find out something about it," Larry insisted.

At that moment, a shout came from the slope below them. "Hey, you up there!" a rough voice called. "Get off that hill!"

The four young people whirled around. A surly-looking man on horseback was staring up at them from the base of the mountainside.

"Porfirio!" Linda gasped. "But he doesn't own any horses, according to Señor Rincón!"

"He could have rented one," said Kathy. "But why would he come out to this deserted place?"

"I have an idea!" Bob exclaimed softly. "That matador business may just be a cover-up for some crooked work he's carrying on!"

"You heard me!" the man yelled again. "Get off that mountain. It's dangerous—full of holes and landslides. No one is allowed to go up there."

"What runs through this pipe we see?" Linda called down to him.

The man gave a black look from under his heavy brows. "I don't know anything about a pipe. It's probably an old one that's been around for a long time. Well, are you going to leave or shall I use force to knock some sense into you?"

"We saw you at the Tijuana bullfights yesterday, remember?" Bob ventured, stalling for time. "That was a great performance you put on."

"You didn't see me," the man barked. "I wasn't there. Now get going!"

"He's really off his rocker," Kathy whispered, "unless he's a good actor playing two parts."

"And one of them sinister," Larry added.

"I agree," said Bob. "We'd better leave." He spurred his horse, raised his hand in salute, and called, *"Adiós!"*

The others gathered up their reins. "Let's spot as many landmarks as we can," Linda urged. "I'd like to come back to investigate this pipe."

Bob led them off in a line slanting down the mountain. As if satisfied that they were leaving, the man turned and galloped off in the opposite direction. When he was out of sight, the four riders started up the slope again.

After making their way through an area of dense, matted, prickly brush, the Old Sol foursome came out onto a section of rocky formation.

"There's the place we ate our lunch the other day," Kathy remarked.

Exhausted, the riders slid from their saddles. They ground-hitched the horses and loosened their cinches.

"How did that Porfirio fellow think he could get away with denying he was at the bullfight?" Larry asked as he took off his big hat and fanned his face.

"Maybe he isn't quite bright, as Kathy suggested," Linda mused. "But I'm convinced he's mixed up with Barco in some way—and that Barco's involved in the disappearance of Agua Vieja!"

"We haven't gotten anywhere proving that theory," Bob said in disgust.

"But we must try to fit all the pieces together," Linda insisted.

"That's true," Larry said. "And I think the pipe and the fact that Porfirio was so disturbed about our being on the mountain are very important pieces!"

"Also," Linda went on, "that pipe didn't look rusty enough for an old abandoned one."

"Check," said Bob.

Kathy stretched out on a flat rock in the meager shade of a gnarled juniper tree. "Maybe Porfirio is just trying to throw us off his trail by lying about where he has been. He's confusing *me*, all right!"

Larry laughed. "Me, too."

Linda and Bob were poking around among the rocks, stopping every now and then to listen.

"Hear any more voices?" Kathy asked lazily.

"Not yet, but I don't want to miss any," Bob said thoughtfully. "I'm positive that the voice we heard the other day was carried through this rock formation from some distance away. There isn't a hole big enough for a squirrel to hide in around here."

"If we could only figure a way to trace the sound to that point," Linda said, "we might find out what good deed Little Barco was being praised for."

"And if we could find Barco and get him to talk, we might be able to solve the mystery of the water," Bob declared.

At that moment, a burst of loud, raucous laughter startled them. They looked at one another in amazement for a second, scarcely able to believe what they had heard. Then Bob and Larry carefully searched the surrounding area. There was no one around.

Linda motioned the other three to come close to her. Then she murmured, "I've just thought of something. If we could hear that voice from a distance, then our voices could be carried there in the same way."

"You're right, Linda!" Bob said excitedly. "Our conversation was overheard. That was someone laughing at my comment that we ought to find Barco."

"Maybe it was even Barco himself!" Kathy said, her eyes almost popping out of her head in excitement.

"Now that he knows we're looking for him,"

Larry told the others in a whisper, "it's going to make our job extra hard."

"If the laugh was Barco's," Linda reasoned, "then the voice we heard the other day was probably Porfirio's. That would prove that he and Barco are working together on some scheme."

"That's wrapping it up," Bob said with a grin. "So let's eat. I'm famished!"

The four took their packages of lunch from their saddlebags and spread the food out on the rocks. For a few minutes, they ate in silence. Then they began to talk in normal tones. They did not mention the water mystery again.

After a brief rest, Bob sat up. "We'd better be getting back to the ranch," he advised. "The afternoon's going to be pretty hot."

They all took long drinks of water from their canteens, then wrapped up the debris from the lunch and put it in their saddlebags.

As Linda mounted Chica, a wave of dizziness overtook her. She clutched the pommel to keep herself from falling. What's the matter with me? she thought.

To her relief, no one seemed to notice, and she managed to bring up the rear of the procession. It was all she could do to stay in the saddle, and she drooped over the saddle horn.

This heat is really getting me, Linda thought. I guess I should have stretched out for a while the way Kathy did.

Her sensitive mount became aware at once of the lack of a firm hand on the reins. Chica d'Oro grew uncertain of her footing, and this made her gait rough.

Linda wanted to sit up and gather Chica in with her usual expert manner, but she felt too tired to make the effort. She only loosened the horse's reins more as she clutched the pommel.

"I'm sorry, baby," she whispered. "You'll just have to do the best you can. But please, please, don't fall down the hill."

Linda's head ached dully, and each jolt of Chica's descent made it worse. The girl felt as if the ride would never end. They finally arrived at the Quinta Floresta stables, and Linda slid from the saddle, feeling like a sack of meal.

When no big, yellow dog came bounding up, she looked around for him. "Rango! Rango!" she called. There was no response.

Felipe came hurrying up. "Rango has not been here all day. He is not with you?"

"No." Linda shook her aching head. "Oh, Bob, Rango wasn't hiding. Something has happened to him again!"

Her brother was tired and slightly out of sorts. "If that dog can't keep out of trouble, it's his own hard luck. He runs away every time we leave him alone!"

Bob began to unsaddle Rocket. "We can't bother about him now. We have four horses to rub down and feed."

Linda turned back to Chica and slumped against her saddle.

Instantly Felipe was at her side. "You are tired from the long ride," he said kindly. "I will take care of your horse for you. I will treat her very good."

"Thank you, Felipe," Linda said gratefully. "I guess I'll have to let you. I just don't feel at the moment as if I could do it."

"Bad heat," Felipe said sympathetically as he began to unfasten Chica's saddle girths.

Linda dropped down on a stool by the stall to wait for the others. In a few minutes, Kathy came running up to her.

"Are you ill, Linda?" she asked with concern.

"Not really. I think I've just had too much heat."

Patches gave an impatient whinny. She began to stomp her feet. The pinto's saddle was uncinched and evidently she wanted to be rid of the heavy leather on her back.

"Go finish with Patches," Linda said, trying to smile. "I'll wait for you."

Chica d'Oro looked at Linda with questioning eyes, but the filly seemed to be enjoying Felipe's expert rubdown. She whinnied approvingly.

Finally all the horses had been taken care of and their riders filed up to the house. Señora de Santis was waiting for them.

"I hope you had a pleasant ride," she said. "There is a surprise for you—an invitation. It came by telephone while you were gone."

Linda's heart sank. The last thing she wanted to do was go anyplace or meet anyone. All she desired was a cup of hot tea and bed.

"Is the invitation from anyone we know?" Kathy asked, curious.

"It is from friends of Pedro and Josefina," their hostess replied. "They are Ivan and Kristin Syskoi from Colonia Catarina. They have invited you four to visit them in the colony for a few days."

"Where is Colonia Catarina?" Kathy inquired.

Señora de Santis explained that it was a small Russian village in the hills. It had been settled by a group of religious emigrants from Russia called Dukhobors. Their religion was based on the belief that all men are brothers and equals. They therefore refused to acknowledge any worldly ruler.

"They are very high-type people," she continued, "and cause no trouble. For this reason the Mexican government allows them to live in their colony and follow their own dictates."

"They sound very interesting," Bob commented. "I'd like to see the place."

"I am sure you will find your visit pleasant," Señora de Santis remarked. "I am happy that you are to have this opportunity. The older people in the colony still speak Russian, but the younger ones have learned English and Spanish."

"It sounds fascinating," Linda said hesitantly, trying to think of an excuse without mentioning her illness. "But—but I don't think Chica should take such a long trip after our ride today."

"Oh, my dear, you could not go by horseback," their hostess said. "You would drive there in your car. The village is forty miles from here."

Linda smiled wanly. "That's fine, then. If you will excuse me, I think I'll go to bed. I don't care for any dinner."

"Linda got a little too much sun today," Kathy explained when their hostess looked concerned.

"I am so sorry," Señora de Santis said sympathetically. "Get into bed immediately and I will have María bring you some broth."

"Thank you," Linda said. "I'm sure I'll feel fine in the morning. The trip sounds wonderful!"

But to herself, as she sank onto her bed, Linda said, Am I going to be ill? Will I have to miss the trip?

The Russian Village   12

Linda slept fitfully. She was awakened by the sound of Kathy bounding out of bed and pulling up the venetian blinds.

"It's a super-duper morning!" Kathy cried. "Just the day for a visit to 'Russia in Mexico'! Are you awake, Linda?"

The other girl dragged herself to a sitting position. "I am now," she replied with a wry smile.

Kathy sobered a bit. "How do you feel this morning?" she asked solicitously.

"Oh, I'll pull through," Linda said, sinking back against her pillow again. "I'll get up in a minute."

"Take it easy," Kathy advised. "I'll have my shower first and be out of your way." Then she disappeared.

Oh, if I just didn't have to leave this bed! Linda thought. But she knew that the others would not go to Colonia Catarina without her, and this was too good an opportunity to miss in connection with the written report to the Youth Council. Moreover, she did not want to disappoint Ivan and Kristin, who had probably made preparations for them.

Kathy whirled from the shower, put on her clothes, and left, saying that she would meet Linda at the breakfast table. By the time Linda had bathed, donned a bright cotton dress, and brushed her dark hair until it shone, she felt better.

When she reached the portico, the others were eating breakfast. "Did Rango come back?" Linda asked as she slipped into her place.

"Not yet," Bob replied. "But please don't worry. He returned the other time, and I'm sure he will again. No one can keep him when he doesn't want to stay."

Linda did not feel so confident. She was certain that Rango had been stolen again. And this time, the guilty person would take extra care that the dog did not escape!

She did not wish to express further alarm, feeling that the de Santises had enough on their minds at the moment. The rancher had reported increasing signs of wilt on the olive trees.

Linda ate a light breakfast, then went in search of Felipe. She found him in the stable yard after she had spoken to Chica d'Oro.

She said to the *vaquero*, "If Rango comes back, will you please tie him up by Chica's stall and give him some food and water?"

"I will do that, *señorita*," he promised.

A little later, when Linda and Kathy came to the front door ready for the trip, they saw the Old Sol station wagon parked in the driveway. It had been freshly washed and polished.

"Did you do that beautiful job this morning?" Linda asked Bob and Larry.

The boys grinned proudly. "Of course!" Larry said. "*We* don't stay in bed after sunrise!"

Linda smiled. "How about rainy days?" she teased.

Señor and Señora de Santis came to the door to bid their guests good-bye. "Here are the directions for finding the Russian village," the rancher said, handing Bob a sheet of paper.

The young people waved farewell and drove out to the highway. Linda had been relieved that they were traveling by car rather than on horseback. But now her head began to throb, and she wished that she were on Chica out in the open air.

Kathy, Bob, and Larry kept up a merry banter. Finally Kathy turned to Linda. "You haven't said a word. Are you still worrying about Rango?"

Larry, who was seated in front with Bob, turned around. "I still think he has a playmate somewhere and goes off to see him. It might even be that *peón's* dog!" Then, looking more closely at Linda, he asked quickly, "Are you all right? Do you want to turn back?"

"Of course not." Linda forced a smile. "It's just a headache. I'll get something for it when we arrive at Colonia Catarina."

Following Señor de Santis's directions, Bob turned off the highway onto a dirt road. They followed this for some time as it twisted and turned through the mountains. Then, rounding a bend, they looked down into a bowl-shaped valley. A road ran through the center of it, and on either side were small, yellow houses with softly mellowed, blue roofs.

Linda was enchanted by the sight in spite of her aching head. "Could you take a picture of the village from here, Larry?" she asked. "I'd like to make a painting of it when I get home."

Bob pulled the car to the side of the road, and Larry jumped out. He took several snapshots of the valley and the rows of houses. "It's a little far away for a really good picture," he said apologetically as he climbed back into the car, "but maybe these will be clear enough to jog your memory, anyway."

Bob drove down the road, which wound into the valley. When they reached the village, Kathy exclaimed at its spotlessness. Even the wide, hard dirt road that formed the main street looked as if it had just been swept.

The few people about stopped and smiled at the

visitors as the car went by. The men wore beards. The neatly attired women had on snowy-white aprons and caps lavishly trimmed with lace.

"They look like big dolls," Kathy remarked.

"This must be the general store," Bob said, pulling to a stop by the board sidewalk. "I'll go there and inquire where we can find the Syskois."

As he stepped from the car, a tall boy and girl who had been standing by the store came toward him. They were both blond and blue-eyed.

"You are the de Santises' friends from California?" the boy asked.

When Bob introduced himself, they told him that they were Ivan and Kristin Syskoi. Larry and Kathy jumped out to shake hands with them.

Linda lay back in her seat. She felt too ill to move. When Kristin opened the door to speak to her, she said quietly, "I'm very sorry not to be more sociable, but I feel dreadful. Will you take me to a doctor, please?"

Kristin looked at Linda with tender sympathy. "We have no doctors here, but we will take you to our nurse woman, Madame Poltava."

"Thank you," Linda murmured gratefully.

Kristin and Kathy sat in the back seat with Linda, while the three boys crowded in front. Ivan directed Bob to the first dwelling outside of town. Actually, this consisted of two small houses connected by a breezeway and set on a knoll.

As soon as the car stopped, a woman hurried

outside. She had large, strong features and graying brown hair twisted into a knot under her cap. Her clothes were crisply starched.

Kristin quickly stepped from the car. In English, she said, "Madame Poltava, these are friends from the States, Linda and Bob Craig, Kathy Hamilton and Larry Spencer. Linda is feeling ill."

"I am happy to meet you all," Madame Poltava said, smiling. She put out her hand to Linda. "Come with me, my dear." When Linda took the woman's hand, she felt a soothing strength in it that gave her immediate confidence.

Madame Poltava spoke to Kristin. "Take your friends into my house and show them around. I will care for Linda."

"Thank you, madame," Kristin said. She motioned the others to follow her. "You'll love her art treasures," she assured them.

The woman led Linda into the other building, which proved to be a two-room infirmary. There were four cots in one small room, and in the other a long, scrubbed table and cabinets of instruments and medicine bottles.

Almost before Linda realized what was happening, she was in a cool muslin gown and Madame Poltava was tucking her between smooth sheets on one of the cots.

"What's the matter with me?" Linda asked. "What do I have?"

"It isn't anything very serious, my dear," the

nurse replied reassuringly. "You have what many tourists get. It is caused by overexertion, worry, the heat, and food and water to which you are not accustomed."

As she spoke, the nurse had prepared a powder in a small glass of water. "Drink this." Then she handed Linda a pill and another glass of water.

Linda lay back. A feeling of relief and restfulness swept over her.

When she awoke some time later, her headache was gone, but she still felt very tired. She wanted just to lie quiet for a while. Her door had been left open a few inches for better ventilation, and she heard the sound of voices in the next room.

By moving to the edge of the cot, she could see that Madame Poltava was changing the dressing on the hand of a fieldworker. After that, Linda watched as the woman cleaned a boy's badly skinned knee and put a bandage on it.

A few minutes later, a girl of about twelve came into the room leading a tearful four-year-old. Linda heard the girl explain that her little sister had run a thorn deep into her arm.

The nurse lifted the child to the table, talking to her all the while. In a few seconds, the youngster was smiling. Madame Poltava then brought down a jar of candy from the shelf and gave each girl a piece. Now she cleaned and examined the little one's arm.

"I'll have to cut this a bit in order to reach the

thorn," she said to the older girl. "You must hold your sister's arm still."

The girl's eyes grew round, but she did not reply. The nurse anesthetized the arm, then directed, "Now, Mala, hold her arm firmly."

Mala hesitated. The she cried out something in Russian and ran out the door.

"Mala, Mala!" screamed the small child. She would have jumped from the table except for the nurse's restraining hand.

Quickly Linda leaped from her bed and went into the other room. "I'll hold her arm," she volunteered. Then, seeing Madame Poltava's uncertain look, she smiled. "I feel much better. I'll be glad to help. I've had a course in first aid."

Linda turned to the little girl and said smilingly, "Hello, honey." The child was so surprised and interested in the newcomer that she stopped screaming. "Will you let me hold your arm?" Linda went on. "Madame Poltava won't hurt you, and wouldn't you like to see the thorn when she pulls it out?"

The child smiled through her tears. Had she understood? She let Linda hold her arm while the nurse deftly removed the thorn. When she held it up in the pincers, the little girl laughed in delight. It was a matter of only a few minutes until the wound was dressed and the patient delivered to her older sister.

Madame Poltava turned to Linda. "Thank you,

my dear. You were heaven-sent. But back to bed for you. You may feel better, but I'm sure you're very weak."

Linda laughed. "How did you guess?" She gratefully returned to her cot.

A short while later, the nurse came in and sat down to talk. "I sent your friends on to the Syskois' house. They will have supper and music and folk dancing in the family's big kitchen afterward. They will spend the night there, but I think it is best that you stay here with me. In the morning, you will feel strong again, I'm sure."

Linda smiled fondly at the woman. "You are a miracle healer."

Madame Poltava looked solemn. "Only so long as my medical supplies hold out." Then, at Linda's questioning look, she explained, "Our village is a poor one. Very few of the people can afford to pay much, if anything, for medical aid. They all tithe to the church, and from it I receive a small regular amount of money, but that is all."

"And *you* have to live too," Linda murmured.

"Oh yes. The men are very kind and work my small farm for me. My produce is taken to market along with the rest. I give what I can for things needed here, but there is a constant lack of proper medical supplies."

Linda had an inspiration. "Back home," she said, "clubs or groups of people sometimes put on entertainment to raise funds for a worthy cause. Perhaps my friends and I could have a little fiesta and make some money to help you buy supplies. Of course, I would have to consult our hosts, Señor and Señora de Santis."

Madam Poltava clasped the girl's hands and exclaimed, "What a blessing that would be!" Then she stood up. "I will cook supper for us now. You need not dress. I will bring you a robe. There will be only the two of us."

She took a crisp cotton wrap and a pair of straw slippers from a drawer and handed them to Linda. The girl put them on and walked with the nurse through the breezeway into her living quarters. Here there were two rooms in front, each with a long table and benches and with chairs lining the walls. In the rear of the house were a kitchen and a bedroom.

Noticing Linda's look of surprise at the two sets of tables and benches, Madam Poltava smiled. "We have all our Dukhobor meetings and village get-togethers here."

Linda walked around the two rooms admiring the Russian art objects on display. There were somber portraits painted on wood, elaborate vases, and several of the Russian "Easter eggs" made of delicate porcelain, exquisitely decorated.

"There will be a feast here tomorrow," Madame Poltava told Linda as they sat down to their simple supper of boiled lamb shanks and turnips. "You will find that all the conversation will be in Russian, but the younger people speak English and Spanish also."

"Your English is very good," Linda said.

"I studied medicine in England when I was young," the woman replied. "Then I married and returned to Russia, but came here later with my husband. I have been a widow for three years."

"Do you treat all the ailments in the settlement?" Linda asked her.

"Not entirely. Our bonesetter is also our boot-maker," Madame Poltava said, to the girl's amaze-ment.

Linda went to bed early. She was awakened the next morning by pounding on the door of the infirmary. Looking out the window, she saw a young Mexican boy. He was holding the halter of a burro with a bad wound on its neck.

"Nurse woman! Nurse woman!" the boy called in Spanish.

Madame Poltava hurried from her house and led the boy and the donkey inside the infirmary. Linda dressed quickly and joined them, eager to watch.

"The mountain lion that killed a steer attacked my Reynaldo," the boy was explaining.

"If the mountain lion killed a big steer, how did the little burro escape death?" Linda asked him.

He did not answer, but as Madame Poltava put disinfectant and a medicated salve on the wound, she explained. "Many Mexicans will tell you it is because the burro has the sign of the cross on its back. See the dark line down the middle and across each shoulder?"

When the boy and his Reynaldo had left, Madame Poltava and Linda had a breakfast of sweet rolls, coffee, and milk. They had just finished eating when the Old Sol station wagon drove up and the five other young people ran into the house. They were delighted to find Linda feeling well again.

"It's all due to Madame Poltava's wonderful care and medication," Linda said, giving the nurse a warm smile.

When her benefactress went into the infirmary, Linda told Bob, Kathy, and Larry of the woman's selfless devotion to the sick of the colony, and its great need for adequate medicines.

"I thought we might put on a benefit fiesta at Quinta Floresta and raise some money for medical supplies," she concluded.

"What a neat idea!" Kathy said enthusiastically.

"Sure is!" Bob and Larry agreed.

With glowing eyes, Kristin said, "That is very kind of you. And Ivan and I could come over and help."

Just then, Madame Poltava joined them, and Kathy bubbled over in praise of Linda's riding and her beautiful palomino, Chica d'Oro. "If Linda puts on a show, you can be sure it will be a grand success."

The nurse smiled. "Then I hope the fiesta will be held," she said.

Madame Poltava now handed triangular scarfs of lace-trimmed, white linen to Linda and Kathy. "You must wear these on your heads when we go to the church. The service starts in a few minutes," she explained.

The group walked down to the center of the village, where the rectangular church stood. As they filed into the building with the smiling Russians, Linda noticed rows of raised benches along each side, with a few at the end. Presently the men of the congregation took their places on one side, while the women seated themselves on the other. Madame Poltava motioned the young people to the end benches, which Linda assumed were meant for visitors.

In the center of the church on a high oak stand stood a beautiful brass and cloisonné samovar. As the church members arrived, they looked into it and said a brief prayer before taking a seat.

"I'd like to know what's in there," Kathy whispered.

Linda, too, was curious. "I'll ask Madame Poltava when the service is over," she said.

The religious service proceeded. A number of the older men rose and spoke in Russian. Between each two speeches, the women sang an a cappella chant.

When the service had ended and the congregation was leaving, Linda told Madame Poltava of the girls' desire to know what was in the samovar.

"Of course," she replied. "Go up and look in."

Linda was the first to peer inside the old urn. She turned away with a puzzled expression on her face.

A Surprise Performance 13

"Why, it's only an old, gray stone," Linda said, surprised.

The others pressed forward for a look into the samovar. They appeared equally puzzled.

Madam Poltava smiled. "That stone is one of the most valuable relics in the world," she said. "It is worth a fortune."

It doesn't look it! Kathy thought.

"I will tell you the story," the Russian woman said. "That old, gray stone was found here. On it is carved the earliest date yet to be discovered in the Western Hemisphere, the Mayan equivalent of 291 B.C."

"Amazing," Linda said, greatly impressed.

The woman sighed, then continued. "Its sale would bring a lot of money to this colony. But the stone will not be sold—we believe it to be sacred and that it ensures our peaceful habitation here. Our relic is carefully guarded—several attempts have been made to steal it."

"How awful!" Linda cried.

Madame Poltava suddenly gave the visitors a broad smile of contentment. "So you see, as long as we keep the stone safely here, life treats us well!"

The young people laughed and walked back to her house, where the feast would be held. All the Syskoi family and many of their relatives came for the festivities. The men had changed to loose, red cotton blouses with brightly embroidered sashes.

"The cooking will take place outdoors," Kristin explained.

The men soon had a hot fire burning in the garden fireplace. Every guest added a contribution to the huge, iron soup kettle—gallons of beef stock, shredded beef, various root vegetables, and plump, red tomatoes.

When it was ready, the food was carried indoors to the long tables. In addition to large bowls of the hearty, delicious soup, there were plates heaped with slices of creamy goat cheese, loaves of crusty bread, and big, glazed cookies.

The men sat at the table in one room, while

the women ate in the other. The door between was closed.

Linda asked Kristin the reason for this. "It is so there may be separate man and woman talk," the Russian girl told her. "Perhaps you think this is a strange custom, but it gives all of us a chance to talk about the others!"

Linda and Kathy giggled, then Kathy asked, "Do you and your brother plan to remain here in the colony?"

"Yes, we do," Kristin replied emphatically. "Ivan is a good farmer and likes it. Each day, the older men grow less able to run the farms, so the younger ones must take their place. They are introducing more modern methods. She smiled. "I like it here, too."

Linda smiled in return. "I also like it here, but how do you communicate with the outside world?" She had learned from Madame Poltava that there were no telephones in the colony. "And how can we get in touch with you about the benefit fiesta?"

"There is a phone in the market up on the highway," Kristin informed her. "I will write that name and number down for you. You can call the market and leave a message. Someone will deliver it to me, then I will call you back."

"Fine."

When the meal was finished, the door between the rooms was thrown open. Then, under the leadership of a fine-looking old man with a long, white beard, the crowd began to sing Russian folk songs. The Old Sol group could not understand the words, but they were able to hum the familiar melodies.

"Wasn't that fun?" Linda said as the festivities ended.

The sun was low in the west when the four visitors finally said their thank-yous and good-byes to the Syskois and Madame Poltava.

"We'll see you soon!" Linda called to Kristin and Ivan when the station wagon began to move off down the main street.

"What a grand experience!" Kathy said with shining eyes as they drove out of the valley. "We'll have pages and pages in our Youth Council note-books."

Later, with Colonia Catarina far behind, as the wagon was skirting one of the big Mexican ranches, Linda suddenly pointed across a field. Two large, light-colored dogs were racing away from a man on horseback. He was twirling a lasso. The next instant, the rope snaked out and dropped around the feet of the dog in the lead.

"Look!" Linda gasped. "Isn't that other dog Rango?"

Immediately Bob pulled the station wagon to the side of the road, and everyone jumped out. The rider had turned and now saw the group. He leaped to the ground, picked up the lassoed dog, and swung him across the front of his saddle. Then he quickly mounted and galloped off in the opposite direction.

"Good night!" Larry gasped. "That's a new kind of sport!"

"I'm sure that other dog is ours!" Linda insisted. "Rango! Rango!" she shouted.

The dog swung around. Recognizing Linda and the others, he stretched his great limbs in a mad dash toward the road. Just before Rango reached the station wagon, he collapsed on the ground, and the Craigs dashed forward.

Linda was on her knees beside the dog the next second. "Rango!" she said in distress. "What happened to you this time?"

The big dog was in bad shape. His hair was matted from moisture and dirt. Patches of it were missing as though torn off in some desperate effort to escape from confinement.

Linda looked up at Bob and Larry. "You see, he *wasn't* hiding from us or running around having fun. He was *dognapped*—and he's been mistreated!"

Bob knelt and ran a gentle hand over Rango. "I know, Linda, but there was nothing we could do about it at the time. I wanted you to enjoy your visit to the Russian village without worrying."

Mollified, Linda smiled at her brother. "Okay," she said, "but we'll keep Rango shut in the utility room until we find out what this is all about, or until we return home."

"Agreed!" Bob replied.

Rango raised his head then, and they saw that he held something in his mouth.

"What have you there, boy?" Bob asked, and put out his hand.

When Rango dropped the object, Linda and Bob examined it carefully. It was a torn piece of leather about three inches long and four inches wide. The piece was lined with canvas and stitched into small squares.

"Rango has brought us a clue!" Linda exclaimed. She patted his head. "Good boy! But how I wish you could talk and tell us what this is and where you got it!"

Kathy and Larry had joined the Craigs and looked at the torn bit. Larry remarked, "I'm sure this has some significance in our jigsaw puzzle, but at the moment I can't see where it fits in."

Kathy looked around nervously. "That roughrider might come back and try to get Rango again. I suggest we move on!"

"No argument!" Bob said. "If this leather is a piece of evidence against him, he'll be mighty eager to get it back. He may return with a gang!"

"I wonder who he is," Larry said. "Porfirio?"

Linda shook her head. "No. I'm sure of it. He is shorter than the matador, but he was too far away to see plainly."

As soon as the four young people arrived at Quinta Floresta, Bob put Rango in the utility room and brought him food and water. The dog dropped exhausted to the pad and feebly licked Bob's hand.

There was much to discuss before dinner was served. Señora de Santis observed, "What a blessing it was that you came past that field in time to rescue Rango!"

"He was really worn out," Bob said, "but I'm sure he would have made it back here before he dropped."

Señor de Santis was examining the oddly lined piece of leather. "This is indeed a curious fragment," he remarked.

"It might be a piece from a horse collar," Larry guessed.

"Or a dog collar," Bob mused.

"That's it!" Linda exclaimed. "Remember the *peón* we believe to be Little Barco mentioned Rango's big neck and seemed eager to buy him for that reason. He wanted to use him for some special purpose that had to do with a dog collar!"

"It looks as though something might have been hidden in these little pockets," Señor de Santis suggested.

Linda said excitedly, "I wonder if it was some sort of contraband that could have been carried by Rango without anyone's suspecting what was going on."

"That's something else we must ask Little Barco when we find him," Bob remarked.

"And now tell us what kind of time you had with

the Syskois," Señora de Santis said. "Did you enjoy Colonia Catarina?"

"Oh, yes!" the four chorused. They related the happenings of their interesting two days.

Linda told the de Santises about her illness and quick cure. Then she described Madame Poltava's primitive infirmary and her need of medical supplies.

"She must be a remarkable woman," Señora de Santis observed.

Linda hesitated a moment, then ventured her idea. "We would like to give a benefit fiesta to raise money for the infirmary. Would you both approve?"

"It's a splendid idea," Señor de Santis answered.

"Indeed it is," his wife agreed. "I am sure the fiesta would be a great success. Everyone in this area admires the Russian colony. The people are so good—they never make any trouble. I think it would be an excellent plan to have the fiesta here at Quinta Floresta, don't you, Enrique?"

"Yes," Señor de Santis said quickly.

Everyone began to make plans. They voted to hold the fiesta the following Wednesday. A nominal admission fee was to be charged, and free entertainment would go on continuously.

There would be three different snack bars. One would sell Mexican *taquitos*, cactus candy, and lemonade. The second would serve American frankfurters and coffee, while the third would have Russian pastries and goat's-milk cheese.

"And let's have some games of skill," Señor de Santis proposed. "I know that several of my friends would be glad to run them and provide prizes."

"Wonderful!" Linda agreed. She turned to Kathy and the boys. "We can manage the hot dogs, can't we?"

"Sure!" Bob and Larry both replied.

"My kitchen help will provide the Mexican food," Señora de Santis offered.

"And I'm sure Kristin and Ivan would bring the Russian pastries," Kathy remarked.

"We four can ride our quadrille for part of the entertainment," Linda said.

"And you and Chica must put on your act!" Kathy declared.

The plans progressed with mounting excitement. Señora de Santis said that she would arrange for Spanish music and dancing, and Linda decided to ask Felipe to contribute some *charro* riding spectaculars.

It was late by the time the discussion ended and everyone went to bed. The next morning, Linda put in a call for Kristin through the highway market. While waiting to hear from her, Linda and Kathy obtained paper and paints from Señora de Santis. They spread them out on a table in the portico and hastily made up a group of colorful posters advertising the fiesta.

When the placards were dry, the boys took them

out to tack on trees and fence rails along the roads. They also drove into Ensenada and were permitted to place a few in shopwindows there.

Shortly after noon, Kristin called. She was delighted when Linda explained their plans for the fiesta.

"Everyone in our village will want to help in some way," she said. "The women can make the pastries, and several of the young men are very good at Russian dances."

"That's perfect!" Linda said happily. "I just know this is going to be the best fiesta ever!"

Next, she went out to the stables and told Felipe about their idea. "Will you and some of your friends put on a few *charro* acts?" she asked. "I'm sure you would be the hit of our fiesta."

Felipe beamed and threw out his chest. "You can count on me, Señorita Linda," he boasted. "We will make a big entertainment for you."

Linda now made a request about a special ride for herself. With a pleading smile, she asked, "Would you show me that *charra* act the lady riders do? I'd like to include it in our fiesta performance."

"Sure!" Felipe cried. "But not on your pretty parade horse. It would not be good for her to slide on her heels. You use my horse."

"But I thought it could be sort of a grand finale to my act on Chica," Linda objected.

"Well, then," Felipe said, "we will do it this way:

I will have my Padillo ready. You quick get off Chica, put on sombrero and serape, mount Padillo, and make the *charra* run."

"Yes—that would be fine!" Linda exclaimed. "I'll have to get a sombrero and a serape, though."

"I have them." Felipe ran into his quarters and brought out the articles. The wide-brimmed hat was decorated with black velvet. Little, silver bells dangled from the huge brim. The serape was striped in red, yellow, and green.

Felipe set the sombrero on Linda's dark hair and draped the serape over her shoulder. He stood back and surveyed her admiringly. "Now you are a beautiful *charra!*" he said.

"Thank you, Felipe," she said. "This is going to be a lot of fun. But please don't say anything about it. I want to surprise everyone!"

"I will not tell. First you must learn the trick, but you will not ride sidesaddle. We will use your saddle so you fit well in it."

He saddled up his horse and showed her the ride—the quick start on the fast run, the long, sliding stop on the heels, the top spin, then the triumphant fast ride off.

"For the spin, you give the horse a couple of quick taps on the rump with this small bat," he explained.

"Let me try now," Linda begged. She laid aside the sombrero and serape, and Felipe helped her to mount Padillo.

After the second try, Linda had mastered the ride.

"Once more," Felipe urged. "Then you will be ready."

Linda raced Padillo forward, then pulled him into the long slide. But as she tapped him for the spin, the latigo strap gave way.

The saddle slipped. Linda was headed for a nasty tumble!

The Secret Tunnel   14

Linda had felt the first rend as the latigo strap had
given way. At the instant her saddle flew off, she
grabbed Padillo's mane, and by holding on tightly
broke her fall.

She let go, caught her balance, and stepped away
from the horse, which was whinnying and steadying
himself after the sudden yank on his mane. I'm
lucky—just plain lucky, Linda told herself.

Felipe, frightened, had raced forward to assist the
girl. "You are hurt, *señorita?*" he asked, taking her
arm and leading her farther from Padillo.

"I—I'm all right, Felipe. The latigo gave way."

The *vaquero* quieted his horse by patting the
animal's neck and walking him around a bit. Then

he said, "I will put on the new latigo. Do not worry, *señorita*. You will make a good ride."

"Thank you, Felipe."

She left him and returned to the house. Before going to her room to change her clothes, Linda stopped at the utility room to see how Rango was. When she pulled open the door, he stopped pacing back and forth and looked inquiringly at her.

"I'm sorry you have to stay in here, old fellow," Linda told him, "but it's for your own good. Maybe I can manage to take you for a run tomorrow—a long one."

The run Linda had in mind was indeed a long one. She wanted to go back to the mysterious mountain and investigate. She felt that Rango, with his keen eyes and sense of smell, might discover some clue that the Craigs and their friends had overlooked. Linda gave her pet an assuring hug, then went to dress.

Since Kathy and the boys were not around, she decided to try finding Señor de Santis. Linda saw him talking to Felipe at the edge of an olive grove. To her dismay, she noted that the leaves on many of the trees away from the watered area were wilting. Their owner's expression was worried.

He is such a good sport to have us here and be so cheerful, Linda thought.

When she walked up, he and Felipe smiled as if there were no problem. At once the rancher said, "I have spoken to my friends and all arrangements for the game booths at your fiesta have been made. We will have some fine prizes."

"Oh, thank you, *señor*!" Linda said gratefully. "Now that everything is set, we'll have time tomorrow to do a little more investigating at the rock mountain. Is it all right?"

"What do you have in mind?" her host inquired. "I thought you had looked around pretty thoroughly."

"I'm sure there's a hollow somewhere among those rocks, because we've twice heard sounds coming from inside them," Linda explained. "I've been thinking that if we could break through the rocks in the area from which Agua Vieja used to flow, we might learn the answer to the mystery."

Señor de Santis gave the girl an approving look. "That is a very good idea. I, too, would like to have a look at those rocks again. But it would be a difficult task to break through them."

He turned to Felipe. "Do you know how it could be done?"

The *vaquero* smiled. "*Sí*," he replied with confidence. "I would use a big hammer!"

"Such a method will require a lot of strength," his employer warned.

Felipe flexed his muscles. "I am strong!" he said boastfully.

"Bob and Larry would be glad to help, I'm sure," Linda suggested.

"Very good," said Señor de Santis. "We will make an expedition to the mountain again the first thing in the morning."

Linda hurried off to tell the others. She found them on the flagstone terrace in front of the ranch house, where the musical and dancing numbers of their entertainment would be given.

"This fiesta is going to be a circus!" Kathy exclaimed happily.

"I don't see any performing animals!" Larry said, teasing her.

"Here's one," Bob said. "Rango can do his disappearing dog act!"

"Linda looks as if she's dying to say something!" Kathy observed. "Give, Linda! What is it?"

Linda told them about the proposed trip for the next day. "Bob, you and Larry have been elected to the rock-breaking squad!"

"I'm flattered," her brother said with a laugh. "Think you can manage, Larry?"

His friend pretended to stagger under a heavy weight. "I don't know. The only rocks I'm used to are the ones in my head!"

In spite of their joking, the two boys appeared the next morning equipped with chisels and a crowbar that Felipe had given them from the supplies in the ranch toolroom. The *vaquero* took along a sledgehammer on his saddle, while Señor de Santis had another crowbar. Everyone carried a flashlight.

Rango had been released from his prison, and romped happily around the group, eager to get started.

"You stay close to us," Linda commanded him. "We don't want to lose you again."

Rango cocked his big head to one side and gave an understanding bark. When the riders were mounted, he took his place at Chica's heels and followed meekly behind Linda.

When the searchers arrived at their destination, they ground-hitched the horses and prepared for the scramble up the rocky formation to the spot where the four young people had heard the mysterious voice.

"You look like real mining prospectors," Linda observed as the men shouldered their tools and began the ascent.

"Not many people go mining for a voice," Larry quipped with a laugh.

"Where did you hear this voice?" Felipe asked.

Linda pointed out the cluster of rocks near the spot where they had picnicked a few days before. Felipe carefully examined them, then announced, "I think water once flowed down here. We will try this spot. Best to start at cracks."

The Old Solers walked about, peering intently at the gray stone. "Here's a crack," Kathy sang out.

Bob hurried over to her side. "Look again," he

advised. "That's just the trail of a traveling insect. See, it ends here."

"Humph!" Kathy sniffed, and went on looking.

Felipe had paid no attention to this conversation, but had continued to search the rock surfaces. Suddenly he struck his chisel a mighty blow with the sledgehammer. "This is a good place—big crack," he said.

Bob and Larry hurried to help. They pounded at the rock for a long time, but it resisted all their efforts to split it. Finally Felipe straightened up and mopped his face.

"We are not getting anywhere with this one," he said. "We will try another." He searched carefully until he found a rock with a wide crack. He inserted the chisel into it. "This looks very good," he observed.

While the boys joined Felipe in pounding the chisel with their sledgehammers, Señor de Santis went to work with a crowbar, prying under the rocks and rolling away the chunks as they were cracked loose. It was backbreaking labor, and the men were forced to stop and rest at frequent intervals.

Linda and Kathy carried away the smaller rocks while the hole grew wider. Finally, Bob gave a cry. "We've hit it! There's a tunnel into the mountain behind these rocks!"

They all pushed forward for a look. The passageway, high enough to stand in, led straight into the heart of the mountain. Before anyone could say a word, Rango had leaped through the hole and disappeared into the darkness.

"Rango! Wait!" Linda called, but the dog was gone. She quickly snapped on her flash and climbed through the hole after him. Bob was close behind.

Beaming their lights ahead, the Craigs hurried along the tunnel. Kathy, Larry, Señor de Santis, and Felipe hesitated only a minute before plunging in after them.

"Linda," said Bob, "look at the floor. It's all gravel instead of dirt. This means water ran through here not long ago."

"Agua Vieja!" she exclaimed.

Rango's excited barking could be heard in the distance. Linda and Bob stumbled along hastily. The tunnel suddenly widened into a kind of grotto. Here Rango was sniffing and pawing at a low, man-made wall built around a pool. At the far side, a wide stream of spring water poured down into it from the rocks at a fast rate.

Linda turned her light on the wet, glistening rock wall. "The source of Agua Vieja!" she breathed.

Bob had been bending over to examine the pool. Now he straightened up. "And the answer to how it was stolen," he added. "Look, Linda, There's a wide, copper pipe going out of the far side."

His sister spun around. "I see it!" she cried. "Oh, Bob, we've solved the mystery!"

"We sure have," Bob agreed. "And we have a pretty good idea who the thieves are, too."

Linda peered more closely at the pipe. "This looks just like the section of pipe we saw down at that cave-in," she said. "It's the real reason Porfirio tried to chase us off the hill. He wanted to scare us away from doing any investigating."

By this time, the others had reached the grotto. They gazed in astonishment at the water gushing down the rocky wall.

Señor de Santis was particularly moved. "To think that I am probably the only one of all the generations of my family who have lived on Quinta Floresta to see the source of Agua Vieja. And I owe it all to you, Linda, my dear!"

"We're just as excited as you are, *señor*," Linda said modestly. "And it seems that we have also solved the mystery of the disappearance of the water. Look at that pipe! Where do you suppose it goes?"

"I have a good idea," the rancher answered grimly. "To a new neighbor of mine named Díaz, who isn't very friendly. I've never seen him."

"And he hired Porfirio to build the wall to shut off the water to Quinta Floresta!" said Larry.

"But he reckoned without our Linda!" said Kathy proudly. "He didn't know the Old Sol detective!"

"I couldn't have done it without all of you," Linda insisted.

Felipe had been studying the wall. "We can fix

this and get our water back, *señor*," he said eagerly. "I will break down the wall on this side, smash the pipe, and plug the hole with rocks. Then Agua Vieja will flow back into the old streambed of the tunnel."

"And your olive groves will be saved!" said Larry.

"Let's do it at once," Señor de Santis said angrily. "Diverting water is a very serious offense."

"I will get my sledgehammer," Felipe offered, and started back into the tunnel.

"We'll get ours, too," Bob said. "Come on, Larry!" The two boys followed Felipe.

Rango had been sniffing around the grotto. Now he suddenly headed off along the far side of the tunnel, which rose sharply uphill.

"I think he scents a trail," Linda said to Kathy. "Let's see what he has found."

The girls followed the big dog down the narrow passage. But as they rounded a turn, the two friends came to a dead end. Linda pointed to a section where large rocks had recently been cemented together to block an opening.

"This was the entrance those water thieves used until we came looking around, then they closed it!" she exclaimed.

"Which means," Kathy added, "that the person we heard talking and later laughing was right inside this tunnel!"

"Yes, and heard us discussing the mystery."

As the girls swung their flashes away from the blocked area, Linda noticed light glimmering through several crevices in it where the cement had failed to stick. She ran up and pressed her eyes to one of the cracks.

"Come see!" she gasped.

Kathy peered through a chink. On the far side of a small ravine was a well-hidden mountain cabin. Seated on the rickety front steps was the short, stocky *peón* they had seen talking to Porfirio. Little Barco, no doubt. Standing beside him was the matador himself!

"I'm so excited I could burst!" Kathy whispered.

In the meantime, Felipe, Bob, and Larry had returned to the grotto with their tools. In a matter of minutes, they had smashed part of the wall, and water began to gush from the pool through the tunnel.

"Felipe and I will finish the job," Señor de Santis announced. He picked up a sledgehammer. "Everyone run out quickly! The water will fill the tunnel!"

He struck the pipe a crashing blow, and Felipe hurled rocks and mud into the opening.

"The girls!" Bob cried suddenly. "Where are they?"

"I thought they went out with you when you left to get your tools," Señor de Santis said, amazed.

"No."

Bob and Larry began to shout Linda's and Kathy's names. In reply, the girls' voices came faintly from the far end of the tunnel. "Come here quick!"

"We'll get them!" Bob told the men. "You go on out of here."

He and Larry dashed up the incline. When they reached the end of the tunnel, they saw Linda and Kathy standing on rocks looking out through the cracks. Rango was with them, sniffing the earth around him.

"Come on out!" Bob shouted to them.

"Look what we've discovered!" Linda exclaimed.

"No time! Hurry up!" Larry cried. He caught Linda's arm at the same time that Bob grabbed Kathy's, and quickly explained about the rising water.

"There's no chance to escape out this end," said Linda, horrified.

Rango held back, whining. Hastily Bob seized him by the thick hair on the nape of his neck and pulled him along.

But the time the Old Solers reached the grotto, the water was up to their armpits. They had a hard time keeping their footing on the wet, slippery gravel. Rango was swimming, just managing to keep his head above the rushing water, but the swift-flowing stream helped his progress.

"We'd better swim, too," Bob advised as the current swept them along the tunnel.

As the water carried them closer to the opening they had dug, a frightening thought came to Linda. We'll have to swim underwater to get out through that hole! Can we make it without being slammed against the rocks?

Linda's Triumph   15

Linda warned the others to be careful as they prepared to go underwater. Larry volunteered to go first. "You follow me, Linda, and Kathy after you."

He filled his lungs with air, then ducked down. The gushing water carried him swiftly through the hole with only a scraped shoulder. Linda and Kathy emerged directly behind him, rolling down the mountainside a distance but finally picking themselves up.

"Where's Bob?" Linda called fearfully when her brother did not immediately appear.

"Here he is, holding Rango!" Larry answered. Bob explained that the dog had refused to put his head underwater and had to be pushed. They all lay quiet for a couple of minutes to get their breath. Then Rango got up and shook himself violently.

"Hey there! You'll get me wet!" Larry joked.

Señor de Santis and Felipe, who had stared in astonishment, helped the others to a more comfortable spot. "It is very hot," the *vaquero* said. "You will dry quick!"

The rancher heaved a great sigh. "I am glad all of you are unharmed. I was very alarmed for you."

"I didn't feel so calm myself!" Kathy admitted with a grin.

"Come on now, Kathy," Bob protested, "you know that swim was just what you wanted."

Señor de Santis shook his head smilingly. "You Americans, you always joke! But I am most grateful to you all for solving this serious problem of our water." He turned to look at Agua Vieja. The stream had found its old channel at the foot of the mountain and was flowing through it to the cattle lands and olive groves of Quinta Floresta.

Linda sat up. "There's more to the story. You haven't heard what Kathy and I saw through a crack in the rocks at the other end of that tunnel!"

She told them of seeing Porfirio and another man they thought was Barco at the mountain cabin. "It won't be long before they'll discover the water isn't coming out of the pipe," she continued. "Then they'll probably open up that other entrance to investigate. Wouldn't that be the perfect time and place for the police to catch them?"

"You are right," Señor de Santis said excitedly. "I must notify the authorities at once!"

The group scrambled down the rocks to their horses and rode home along the flowing stream. The rancher and his *vaquero* gazed at it in delight.

When Señora de Santis heard the news that Agua Vieja had been restored, she burst into happy tears. "How can we thank you young people enough?" she cried when able to speak again.

Linda put an arm around the woman's shoulders and gave her an affectionate hug. "You've given us such a wonderful time here at Quinta Floresta, we don't need any other thanks."

Señor de Santis phoned the chief and gave him full details of the diverted water, the location of the mountain cabin, and descriptions of Porfirio and his companion. The officer promised to send men out immediately to apprehend the two and any partners when they arrived at the tunnel opening.

"We probably won't hear anything until tomorrow evening," the rancher reported to the others, who were waiting to hear the chief's plans.

Everyone at Quinta Floresta was in high spirits for the fiesta. The next day the Old Solers and many of the ranch hands worked all morning under the direction of Señor and Señora de Santis. They strung colored balloons among the trees and placed benches and chairs around the grounds. A loudspeaker system to announce the various events was set up by a crew of electricians from Ensenada.

When the Craigs, Kathy, and Larry went into the house to luncheon, they saw that their host and hostess had put on their Spanish costumes. "We thought these appropriate for the occasion," said the Mexican woman.

"You look wonderful!" Linda cried as she walked around to admire the details of their dress.

Señor de Santis wore a handsome *charro* suit of golden-brown suede, with silver wolf heads down the sides of the tight trousers. On the back of his bolero jacket was a sunburst of flat crystals and metallic silver braid.

With a smile Señora de Santis said, "Enrique was a caballero in his younger days. He was known as El Lobo."

"A wolf!" Kathy giggled.

Señora de Santis herself wore a long, full-skirted gown with a beautifully embroidered shawl thrown around her shoulders. She had a tall, tortoiseshell comb in her dark hair, with an exquisite, black lace mantilla draped over it.

Luncheon was a hurried affair. They had just finished when a big truck drove into the grounds. In it were Ivan and Kristin Syskoi, Madame Poltava, and a number of their Russian friends. The men had on their red cotton blouses, full, bloomer-like trousers, and high, black leather boots. The women were also in native costume.

"These are the best dancers in our colony," Kristin explained as she introduced them to the Old Solers and their hosts.

Shortly afterward, men, women, and children began streaming through the ranch gates. The refreshment stands were set up and started to do a brisk business. The frankfurter booth, with Kathy in charge, was especially popular.

"Do you think we'll have enough hot dogs?" she anxiously asked Bob, who stood nearby. She fished one out of the boiling water.

"Sure," he replied. "Larry and I bought enough for an army this morning."

At that moment Señor de Santis stepped to the loudspeaker and announced the first event of the afternoon—a riding exhibition to be put on by Felipe and four of his *charro* friends.

Visitors hurried away from the booths and down to the ring behind the stables, where the riding was to take place. The *charros*, in their elaborate costumes, were lined up along one side.

When the crowd had gathered, two of the men stepped forward. They were champion ropers. As the men twirled their lariats in complicated patterns, the spectators cheered wildly. Then the *charros* mounted their horses and did more fancy rope tricks from their saddles.

Bob and Larry watched in fascination. "We'll have to do some practicing when we get back to Old

Sol," Bob observed. "We're way behind these fellows!"

"We'll have something to show Cactus Mac," Larry agreed with a grin.

As soon as the rope tricks were over, all the *charros* put on an exhibition of fast riding with quick stops. The dust rose in clouds as the horses skidded to a standstill.

For a finale to the *charro* riding, one of the rope experts twirled his lariat in a huge loop and lassoed the four others as they thundered past him in a fast run. The audience went wild with applause.

"*Olé! Olé!*" the cheers rang out as the *charros* lined up to take a bow.

The crowd wandered back to the booths and the games. The crackle of rifle fire could be heard as men and boys struggled to hit a target of moving clay pigeons. Children had a wonderful time tossing rubber balls at a paper clown's face.

Linda smiled happily at Kathy. "I think everyone's enjoying it, don't you?"

"If the number of hot dogs I've cooked means anything," Kathy observed, "they're all having a ball!"

"Listen!" Linda said. "Señor de Santis is announcing our quadrille. Come on, we'll have to hurry!"

"But what about this booth?" Kathy asked.

Madame Poltava had been standing nearby. Now

she came up. "I shall enjoy boiling frankfurters and spreading mustard on buns," she said with a laugh. "You girls run along."

"Thank you," Linda said, dashing off.

The Old Sol riders had often performed their drill and went through it this time with perfect accuracy. They received generous applause when they ended by lining up and raising their hats in a salute to the crowd.

As they left the ring, it was announced that Linda Craig, American exchange visitor, and her trick palomino, Chica d'Oro, would perform next. More people came hurrying from all over the hacienda. Soon there was a deep fringe of spectators around the performing circle.

When Linda rode out in her jeweled, green suit with white boots and hat, a chorus of cheers arose from the crowd. Chica, who had been groomed until she shone, stepped forward daintily in her silver equipment.

Bob started the recorded music by which Linda worked. A hush came over the onlookers as she put the palomino through her routine in perfect form. Enthusiastic applause followed every trick.

Her performance over, Linda rode out at a fast canter to where Felipe stood with his horse near the stables. Quickly she changed to the sombrero, threw the serape over her shoulder, and mounted Padillo.

"*Buena suerte!* Good luck!" Felipe cried, giving Linda a big smile as he handed her the bat.

"*Gracias!* I'll need it!"

She raced back into the ring on a fast *charra* run, executed the long, sliding stop, spun the horse beautifully, tapping him with the bat, then galloped out. Tremendous applause, *olés*, and bravos rang out.

Linda had just jumped off Padillo when Kathy and the boys ran into the stable.

Kathy threw her arms around her friend. "Linda, how did you ever dare do it? You scared me out of my wits!"

Bob grinned. "Marvelous, Sis. You said you wanted to make that run, but I didn't think you would!"

"You were great, Linda!" Larry said. "My hat's off to you."

The last performance was a fast Russian dance on the flagstone terrace, admirably executed. This, too, was received with great enthusiasm.

When the fiesta was finally over and the receipts were counted, the Quinta Floresta group learned that they had taken in far more money than they had hoped to do. Linda turned it over to Madame Poltava with the best wishes of the Old Solers and Señor and Señora de Santis.

The nurse's eyes were full of tears as she said huskily, "I shall try to show my deep gratitude by relieving the misery of our sick and injured villagers. I can never express it properly to you."

When the Russian Dukhobors had rolled away in their truck, Linda and the others at Quinta Floresta sank into comfortable chairs on the patio to rest.

But Linda did not sit still long. "I must let Rango out," she said. "The poor dog has been shut up all day."

She had just returned, with Rango bounding happily at her side, when a police car drove up. In the back were three men handcuffed together and a big, tan shepherd dog.

"He's the one we saw in Ensenada!" Linda exclaimed.

At a prodding from the officers, the prisoners and their dog got out. The men stood staring sullenly at the ground. Rango bounded to the animal's side, and it was evident at once from their friendliness that the two were acquainted.

Meanwhile Linda gasped in surprise, "There are *two* Porfirios!"

"That is right," one of the policemen declared. "These men are twins, Fernando and Carlos Porfirio."

Kathy giggled. "No wonder we thought the man was out of his mind! We were talking to first one, then the other!"

"Where did you find these men?" Señor de Santis asked, out of earshot of the prisoners.

"Carlos Porfirio also goes by the name of Luis

Díaz," the officer explained. "He owns a small stud farm and the cabin that you described to us over the phone. We watched the cabin last night and this morning until we saw Díaz and his *vaquero*, Manuel Barco, here, go up to the entrance into the mountain and start to tear out the stones. We nabbed them both then."

The other policeman went on with the story. "It seems that Díaz did not have enough money to bring in a new water supply, which he needed for his land and horses, so he decided to divert yours to his own use. Barco built the wall and installed the pipe."

"Was his brother Fernando, the matador, mixed up in the water theft?" Bob wanted to know.

"We do not think so. But since he was at the cabin, we brought him along. He and Barco are suspected of smuggling jewels across the border, but we have not yet been able to prove this." The policeman looked discouraged.

"Perhaps I have a clue for you," Linda said.

"*Sí, señorita?*" the officer asked in surprise.

"My dog Rango was stolen twice but managed to escape. The second time he brought back a piece of leather dog collar. It's the same kind that this other dog is wearing now."

"That is Barco's dog, Juan," the first officer said, looking puzzled.

"If you take off Juan's collar, I think you may be surprised at what you find," Linda urged.

The prisoners lunged between the police and the dog, but were roughly pushed aside. One of the officers quickly unfastened Juan's collar.

"Look inside the canvas lining," Linda advised.

Everyone watched eagerly while the lining was ripped open. They gasped as a small cascade of unset gems poured out.

The officer turned to Fernando Porfirio. "If you talk now, it may go easier with you at your trial," he snapped.

Fernando worked his lips nervously, then said in a surly tone, "Barco put the gems in the dog collars. I would go to the other side of the border, whistle the dogs over, and remove the gems. Then Barco would call them back again."

He looked at Linda. "Barco stole your dog, not me," he whined.

Barco's cockiness had vanished. He scowled and muttered. "I only took him twice. I sneaked in here other times, but the dog was too hard to catch. After you saw me in Ensenada, I came down here in a fast car to get ahead of you."

"Was it you who set the stable on fire?" Linda asked. "And if so, why?"

"I did not mean to do that," Barco replied. "I tossed my cigarette away, and it landed in some straw at the corner of the building. I could do nothing about it, so I ran away."

"It *was* you we spotted crossing the field that day," Linda declared.

Barco's glare indicated this to be true. Further questioning revealed that Carlos had been the eavesdropper on the visitors' first night at the ranch. Fernando and Barco admitted to trailing Linda and the others in the boat. The men had wanted to learn if the ranch group had a secret rendezvous with the police to report anything they suspected about the Porfirios' activities.

Carlos had stayed in town that day, and it was he whom Linda had questioned in the shop. The horseshoe with the L imprint had come from one of his animals, and the paper bearing the word "Ensenada" had been dropped by him.

Finally, the prisoners were pushed back into the car. Then the policemen turned to Señor de Santis.

"Your troubles are over now," said the first one, "and ours too, thanks to your young American guests. The Porfirios and Barco will go to jail and the dog Juan to the animal shelter."

"Oh, the poor dog!" Linda cried in distress.

Señor de Santis stepped forward. "We would like a big dog like Juan on the ranch. Will you release him in my custody?"

"*Muy bien, señor,*" the officer agreed. He left Juan with his new owner and drove off with the prisoners.

Rango seemed delighted to have his playmate remain. He and Juan began to wrestle with each other.

"To think of those awful men making a smuggler out of Rango!" Kathy said indignantly.

"Yes," said Bob, "but if they hadn't, he couldn't have provided the clue to the gem smugglers!"

Linda dropped down between the two big dogs, hugging them both around the neck. Then she stood up and said to Rango, "Take Juan to meet Chica d'Oro. I'll follow and feed you." She grinned. "It's time for all good show horses and smuggler dogs to eat!"

THE LINDA CRAIG™ SERIES
by Ann Sheldon

You will also enjoy
NANCY DREW MYSTERY STORIES®
by Carolyn Keene